MIRACLES ARE CHOSEN

BY
MICHAEL J. ALSUP

Coastal Winds Publishing House
Port Arthur, Texas

Coastal Winds Publishing House
3167 63rd Street
Port Arthur, Texas 77640

For information contact: Coastal Winds Publishing House
Email: publisher@coastalwindspublishinghouse.co

_____

ISBN: 9780985040390

Publisher: Pamela Joy Licatino, Port Arthur, TX
Editor: Maegan White

Cover design and layout: SeaShore Creations by Design -
                         Pamela Joy Licatino,
                         Port Arthur, TX

_____

Printing and Distribution: Lightning Source

DEDICATION

To my loving wife Lutz Alsup, who stands by me while I write to tell my story. For she understands what it takes to bring an idea to life.

To Father Rodel Faller. For if not for him, this novel would never have happened. His simple words about the cover photograph that I took. "I cannot get this image out of my head," was the inspiration that I needed. "Thank you."

To Reverend Melvin Wiltz. Adding the little push to complete this novel was the inspiration I needed to finish it. Melvin stood next to me and said. "I prayed to our Lord that he may show the path to bring this story to life." I truly believe that he was right.

Traveling to the Albay Province in the Philippines with my wife, the life lessons are immeasurable.

TABLE OF CONTENTS

Copyright
Dedication

- *Chapter One* -

It was early morning and the jungle humidity was on high alert for this time of year. With temperatures hitting 31 degrees Celsius, a cool wind blew across the valley floor making the early summer bearable. As I was getting dressed, I could hear a strong man's voice coming from the front room. Did my mother have someone visiting? Creeping with silent steps along the hallway, I peeked with one eye around the corner to see who she was talking to. What a relief, it was only the television. I stood quietly listening as I watched the weatherman describe a typhoon named Isabella that was making landfall on one of the northern provinces of the Island of Luzon, "The damages at this time is not known or the death toll." As I was listening so intently, I could hear my mother sobbing as she covered her mouth and mumbled. "Lord, I don't know what it is going to take to help those who are suffering. So many lives are taken for just trying to survive in this world."

*****

Being a four-year-old, I was not yet old enough to attend elementary school like the other children in my community. "I'll be so glad when I am five so I can attend school too." My mother smiled when she heard me speaking and continued to work in her small store that contained many items for sale. I enjoyed helping my mother and did as much as I could by sweeping the mango leaves that continued to fall in front of the door. As I stood next to a shelf that contained cans, bottles and cooking supplies, I found myself mesmerized at the words that were printed on every label. My mouth turned upward into a slight smile as I picked up each container. Mumbling to myself, as I read the ingredients, I may have been too loud, because I seemed to be distracting Mrs. Pina, one of our neighbors, who was making a purchase. Looking at my mothers face, I noticed she was giving me a scornful look.

I returned a package to the shelf and a thought came to mind. I wondered how come I can read and yet, I don't go to school? I was in awe. Maybe God has something special for me, a gift.

"Ali, can you go out and sweep in front of the store again? Those leaves just continue to fall no matter how much you sweep the ground." My mother's request pulled me back to reality.

"Yes momma," I responded.

Grabbing the broom, I headed towards the door, and suddenly, the ground started shaking. I looked around with panic. I stood in shock not knowing what to do. I could hear items falling off the shelves for a few seconds, and how it caused quite a mess inside my mother's little store. I saw the alarmed expression on my mother's face.

"What on earth was that?" Mrs. Pina asked.

"Tremors," I said.

Mrs. Pina grabbed her groceries and left. As I stood by my mother, I could tell she was in dismay to see the aftermath of what had just happened. Her store was in shambles. Some of the glass containers were broken. Several of the packages containing flour and other powdered items broke open when they hit the ground, and a white dust covered everything. Releasing a sigh, I returned the unbroken items to the shelves. The cleanup was going to take both of us several hours of wiping and scrubbing the floors. The look on my mother's face, as she cleaned, told me that she was exhausted and disappointed. The items that had broken meant that she had less things to sell and less money for us.

"Momma go inside. I'll finish cleaning the floor," I said.

She smiled and replied, "We're almost done."

"But I still have my chores to do."

With tears in her eyes, my mother said, "They can wait until tomorrow. This won't take me long," I told her, picking up the broom and tucking strands of my dark hair behind my ears, I marched toward my enemy. The leaves that always seemed to gather in the same spot in front of the store sat there waiting for me. "You're next."

As I was sweeping away the leaves, I caught a dark shadow in my peripheral vision growing larger with every step as it came towards me.

Slowing my pace, I spotted Father Bayon walking by. He stopped for a moment to shift the books he had cradled under his arms. Waving my arms to catch his attention, I shouted, "Hello Father!" I hurried over to where he was standing and took his right hand, putting the back side to my forehead to show respect. Looking up at his face, I could see him smiling at me.

"Hello Ali. How are you today?"

"I'm fine, Father. Did you just feel the ground shake?" I asked.

"I did. I think the Mayon is waking up." I noticed the stack of books he was carrying and fixed my eyes on them. "What are your books about?"

"Why, these are books that I use in my sermons."

"Do you have any that I could read?" I asked.

He pondered for a moment. "I don't know. Just how old are you?"

I answered with a soft voice, "I'm four-years-old." I paused for just a moment, "We don't have any books here except for the bible and I have already read that." Raising my head again in order to see the Father's face, I could tell that he was shocked by what I told him.

"You have read the bible?"

I looked back down as if I was ashamed to talk to a grown up. "Yes Father. I read the entire book."

Father Bayon was in disbelief about the conversation. Shuffling the books that were tucked under his arms, he considered everything

I was telling him.

"Did you understand what you read?"

Looking up at the Father again, I answered, "Yes."

"Ali, let me sit down here for a moment and think about what you just told me." Leaning against a mango tree, Father Bayon opened up the worn cover of the bible that he had carried with him for most of his adult life.

"Father, may I sit next to you?"

Smiling, he answered, "Oh please do."

Thumbing through pages, he began asking me questions from the old and new testaments. Without hesitation, I answered all his questions.

After a while, Father Bayon closed his bible and gently rubbed the top cover. He raised his bible to his chest and studied me for several more minutes. Father Bayon rubbed his jaw and placed his bible on top of the other books that he carried.

"Well, I'll be," he said. "I have several books that I kept from my college days. I will bring them to you tomorrow."

With the biggest smile on my face, I said, "That would be wonderful."

*****

The next morning, Father Bayon was at the front gate of our home. My mother saw him standing there and let him into our front yard.

"Hello Father."

"Good morning Christina. Is Ali here?"

"She is," she said, nodding her head.

My mother raised her voice, "Ali, Father Bayon is here to speak to you."

I walked toward the front gate to where they were standing. "Hello Father," I said, taking his right hand and putting the back side to my forehead as I had always done.

"Ali, I brought these two books for you to read."

My mother had a puzzled look on her face. "Why are you bringing her books?" she asked.

Father Bayon looked at my mother and said, "Why, she asked for them."

My mother was completely confused about what she was hearing. She turned and looked at me, saying, "Ali, you don't know how to read."

"Yes I do, momma. I taught myself."

The Father turned the books around so I could see the bindings. "Pick one," he said.

I opened up a world history book and thumbed through the pages. I found a story about the Spanish influence around the world and began to read. Father Bayon looked at my mother.

"She sounds like a college professor reading aloud to a class," he said as I read the entire chapter in a matter of minutes.

I closed the book gently. Waiting for a couple of seconds, I began my explanation of everything I read. My mother's mouth fell open and she could not speak. The Father raised his brow.

Looking down at the floor, I held the book against my chest as if it were the most wonderful thing in the world. I raised my head to see the expressions of the adults that stood in front of me. They looked at each other, their heads lowered, and they locked their eyes on me.

The Father smiled. "Well, I'll be."

My mother covered her mouth with her hands. "I didn't know," she said and turned to the Father, searching for answers. "How is this possible at her age? She has never been to school."

Father Bayon thought about my mother's questions.

"Christina, God has his reasons why he has chosen Ali. In time, she will lead us down the path he wants us to take and only then will we know the purpose of this. After talking with Ali yesterday, I went back to my office and went online. I researched everything that I could find on how a young person her age can read and understand what she has read. After several hours of searching, I couldn't find any logical answers to satisfy my mind. I called the Archbishop in Manila," Father Bayon explained. "After a lengthy conversation, we both agree that no human has had any hand in her ability to comprehend the knowledge that has been placed before her."

I was listening to the Father speaking about me, but I knew deep in my soul that what I had just done was going to change my family for the rest of our lives.

"Ali, I'll leave these books with you so that you may read them when you have the time," said Father Bayon.

"Okay, but you can have them back tomorrow," I said.

Father Bayon seemed a little surprised at my answer. "That's too early."

I looked at the books the Father brought me. "No. I can read very fast. This history book will take maybe thirty minutes and the English Literature will take about forty-five minutes to complete."

Father Bayon stood, amazed. He recollected taking these courses in college. It took a whole semester to read and comprehend what was in the books. But here, standing in front of him, was a four-year-old girl who could go through the books in a matter of minutes.

The Father got up to leave. "I will see you tomorrow," he said.

My mother closed the door. Kneeling in front of me, she locked her eyes with mine. She still had doubts in her mind.

"How is this possible?" she asked me.

I noticed the quizzical look on her face. Shrugging my shoulders, I said, "I don't know."

After the Father left, he looked up towards the heavens as he headed along his way, whispering to himself, "Can this be?"

*****

Sitting at his desk, Father Bayon made a phone call to Father Castillo, a fellow priest from a neighboring town. "I need you to come with me tomorrow to witness a remarkable little girl. She seems to have the gift of knowledge, and she is only four-years-old," he began. After a long conversation, they set up a meeting for both priests to witness something that could not be explained.

*****

The next day, I was in the process of picking up the pile of mango leaves that I had just swept when Father Bayon approached me.

"Hello Ali."

"Hello Father."

"Ali, this is my friend and fellow priest, Father Castillo. I told him about you and your special gift." I took both of their right hands and put them to my forehead.

Father Castillo, a tall, slender, gray-bearded priest contemplated his thoughts. "Ali, Father Bayon tells me that you can read any book and comprehend what you read. Is this true?"

"It's true, I guess."

Father Castillo studied me with wise old eyes. "How old are you?" he asked.

"I'm four-years-old, and my birthday is April, the twenty-fourth, two-thousand-and-eleven." I could see that Father Castillo was squinting his eyes when I looked up at him.

"How did you know that you could read books?"

"When I picked up the only book that we have, the words seemed to just flow. I studied them and began reading to myself. I can't explain it. It just happened."

I excused myself for a moment. My face was hurting from smiling so much. I recovered my posture and retrieved the family bible from our front room. Standing in front of both priests, I began to read it aloud. Father Castillo was amazed.

Putting his hands onto his gray-bearded chin, he thought for a moment. "How long did it take you to read the Holy Book?"

"About one hour."

"Was that the Old or the New Testament?"

"Both."

Father Bayon smiled brightly. "I told you," he said.

Father Castillo was still not convinced.

"May I borrow your book for a moment?" he asked.

I handed the bible to him. He thumbed through the pages, looking at the scriptures. Peering down at me, he asked about certain chapters and verses. He asked about their meanings and effects on human life. I explained, in detail, everything that pertained to the questions. I then went on to remind Father Castillo about the things he'd forgotten.

He remained quiet for several moments. Then, all he could say was, "My, my."

I excused myself again for a moment and returned with Father Bayon's books. "Father, I've finished these two books. Thank you for letting me read them."

Father Castillo saw what I was holding in my hands. "May I look at these?" He opened the English literature book. "I remember taking this course in college. I always had trouble with some of the events of one of the older stories."

Smiling, I looked up at him. "What part?"

Father Castillo thumbed through the book and came to an older story. "This part," he said. Leaning over, he put his long slender finger on a page. I examined it for a moment and began explaining and summarizing the emotions and motivations of the characters. After several more questions about different stories in the book, he closed it gently and handed it to Father Bayon. Opening the world history book, his slender fingers thumbed through the pages in the same manner.

Looking down at me, he said, "Explain about Roman history and what influences it had on our world today." I explained, in detail, about the questions he asked.

"Now let's discuss World War Two," he said. I recalled in detail facts about Germany, Japan, Italy and the final outcome of the war. I also explained about the nuclear results and what effects it has had on the future of humanity.

My mother had just walked out of our house and was heading to her small store when she noticed the two priests speaking to me. Standing next to me, she looked at both men. "What's going on?" she asked. Father Bayon did not waste any time.

"We came by to speak to Ali. Christina, this is Father Castillo."

My mother looked up at him. "How do you do, Father?"

"Fine, thanks."

"Christina, I spoke to Father Castillo about Ali last night and he wanted to meet her in person."

Father Castillo put a hand on my head. I looked up at his face. He said, "This remarkable child has a wonderful gift."

My mother did not comprehend what they were saying. "And what gift is that?" she asked.

Father Bayon said, in a joyful voice, "Why, the gift of knowledge! And at such a young age. She has the mind of some of the smartest people in the world." Father Castillo rubbed the Holy Cross that adorned his body.

"What I have just witnessed... this is truly remarkable," he said.

"Only one in ten billion babies are born with such a brain. We are blessed to know this child and surprisingly, she lives here, in our community." My mother sighed, overwhelmed with emotions. Looking away from us, she rubbed her hands together and muttered,

" We have no money to send her to school."

Both priests looked at each other. "We'll make sure that she gets the proper education," Father Bayon said as he knelt in front of me. "In order to do this right, we will have to take her to the elementary school to have her tested to see if she can move up in grade levels."

Looking up at mother, Father Bayon said, "Christina, may we get your permission?" he paused. "Oh, I am so sorry," he said, returning his gaze to me." Ali, I guess we need to ask you first. Would you like to study books and someday be able to help your family and fellow Filipinos?"

"I would like that very much, but I am not sure how I would help anyone." However, a thought came to my mind. Perhaps I could help my best friend, Minda, with her schoolwork.

Father Castillo knelt in front of me as well. With a big smile on his face, he said, "Someday my child, you will."

Looking toward my mother again, Father Bayon was waiting for a positive answer.

"Christina, what do you say?"

My mother looked at me. "I can't say right this minute. I will have to talk to my husband. He will not be back from his job for a least another week," she told them.

Both priests stood back up. Father Bayon looked down at me and then at my mother. "We understand. May we check on you and Ali in a couple of days?" he asked.

My mother put her hands upon my shoulders. "That will be fine, I should know something by then."

"Father, if you have any other books that I may read, may I borrow some of them?"

"You certainly may. I'd never deny anyone who wants to learn. A mind is a terrible thing to waste," he said.

After both priests had left our home, my mother placed a call to my father's worksite. My father was excited to hear the good news about my gift of knowledge. He gave his blessings for my abilities to be tested.

My mother knelt in front of me. "Ali, are you sure you want to dive into this? Once this starts, there is no turning back."

"I am sure momma. I have to know why I was given this wonderful gift."

My mother made a call to Father Bayon to let him know the good news.

- Chapter Two -

Later that afternoon a messenger stopped at my house and dropped off a box with a lot of books in it. A note was in the top of the box. It read:

"Ali, these are from the elementary school. Study them and let me know when you would like to take the test.

I yelled at the messenger as he began to leave, "Tell Father Bayon I will take the test in a couple of days!" He looked at the box of books and shook his head.

"I'll tell him, but he doesn't like to waste time. Are you sure about taking the test so soon?"

"I am. These will not take long to read."

The messenger got into his truck, and said, "Okay. I'll tell him."

*****

Late the next afternoon, Father Bayon came to our front gate shouting, "Ali, I have some more books from the elementary school!" I greeted him eagerly at the gate.

"Hello Father," I said, pressing the back of his right hand to my forehead.

"Ali, I have a backpack with more books that we would like for you to study. Depending on how much time it takes you, we'll determine when we can get you tested."

I glanced into the backpack. "I'll have these finished by late tomorrow."

With a pleasing smile on his face, he said, "I don't doubt that at all."

"I have finished all the books that the messenger brought last night."

"How long did it take you to read all those books?"

"Not too long, maybe an hour-and-a-half."

"You are a truly gifted child," Father Bayon said. With his arms pulled across his chest, he said, "Well, I have to be getting along. I have a class to teach tonight. I'll be by tomorrow morning to take you to the school. I made an appointment for you to take a special test. I had a talk with the school administrators, and they were astonished that a young child that lives in our community is so gifted. A decision was made. They sent an email to the Department of Education in Manila asking for this special test."

*****

The next morning, Father Bayon, being a punctual man, knocked on our front door at seven a.m. I told my mother that it was Father Bayon.

"He wants to take me to school so I can be tested," I said.

Opening the door, my mother smiled at the Father.

"Good morning, Christina," he said.

"Good morning, Father. I would like to go with Ali to the school."

"By all means, I think parents should take an interest in their child's development."

Closing the front door, the three of us headed off at a brisk pace toward the elementary school administration building. Father Bayon introduced my mother and I to everyone. A student counselor walked up to where I was standing and knelt.

"Ali, I understand that you are quite a remarkable young lady. Are you ready to take this test?"

I smiled politely. "I guess," were the only words I could come up with. They led me to a small room that was off to the side from the principal's office.

"Ali, you have one hour to take this exam," the counselor said as he handed me a letter-sized, sealed envelope, then they shut the door. Staring at the package they had placed in my hands, a thought occurred to me. I had never taken a test before. It couldn't be that hard though. I broke the seal and opened it up to the first page. Writing my name on the paper, I began to read the instructions.

*****

Father Bayon and Christina were pacing back and forth across the principal's office while Ali took the test.

Mr. Rosa, the school principal, asked, "Does anybody know how this young lady developed her extraordinary mind?"

Neither Christina nor Father Bayon could answer that question. Twelve minutes and fifty-two seconds after receiving the test, Ali opened the door. "

"I'm finished," I said as I opened the door. Every administrator in the office stared at me with a look of shock. The entire office personnel began speaking softly to each other.

Someone muttered, "No way can a person her age finish this test in twelve minutes."

I handed Mr. Rosa my papers. He and a school counselor left the room to grade it. Half an hour later, they returned to where we were waiting to hear the results. Mr. Rosa stood in front of the sofa where the three of us sat.

"I checked it twice. Ali made a perfect score. No mistakes or changing of any answers," he said. Everyone began clapping their hands.

My mother gave me a big hug. "I didn't know," she kept saying.

Father Bayon stood in front of us.

"This is just the beginning," he said. "Now you will have to take a high school test. I will get you all the materials that you will need to study for your next exam." With a very large smile on his face, he seemed to know deep down in his soul what was happening here.

My mother and I said our goodbyes to everyone and headed home.

*****

Standing in front of our gate, I could see the pesky leaves had gathered up again.

"Momma, I want to do my chores," I said.

"If you like," she said. I picked up my broom and headed to the leaf pile.

The next morning, Father Bayon arrived in a padyak, (a bicycle with a cart attached). He began unloading several boxes of books. My mother watched from our front window as Father Bayon paid the driver.

My mother opened the front door.

"Good morning Christina. I have the high school books Ali will need," he said.

I heard the Father talking to my mother. Walking into the front room with a towel wrapped around my head, I saw several boxes of books sitting on the floor.

"Good morning Father. Nice day today."

"Why, it's a fine day. Ali, I have all the materials that you will need to take your next test. You just let me know when and I'll set it up."

I opened the boxes. "Today is Wednesday. I'll do this on Friday," I said.

"Excellent. That will give me time to get everything ready."

Late Thursday afternoon, Father Bayon called my mother. We were to meet him at Cabasan National High School on Friday morning at eight a.m.

*****

As my mom and I entered the school administration building, I stared at all the students walking to class. Walking by them, I could hear their voices. "What's that little girl doing here?" they would whisper.

My mom stopped, turned, and knelt in front of me. "Are you sure that you want to go through with this? You have nothing to prove to anyone."

I looked at her, "I do momma. I have to prove this to myself."

Mr. Sanchez, the school principal, came over and introduced himself to me. "Ali, I have a room set up for you. Is there anything you need before you start?"

"I'm fine," I said. He took me to a small room, similar to the last one.

"Ali, you will have one hour to take this test," he instructed and shut the door.

Christina and Father Bayon began pacing the floors. Christina was making strange noises and Father Bayon noticed that she was biting her fingernails. She caught on when she saw everyone staring at her.

"Sorry," she said, "I'm real nervous having my little girl take a high school exit exam."

Father Bayon patted her on her back and said, "It's okay. We understand."

Mr. Sanchez asked the Father, "How did Ali do at the elementary school?"

Holding his rosary beads in his hands, he answered, "She aced the test in twelve minutes."

Mr. Sanchez raised his eyebrows. "My, that's incredible!"

At seventeen minutes and five seconds, I opened the door and handed in my test. I had just answered one hundred and twelve questions that covered every subject that the school offered. Mr. Sanchez and Mr. Rodriquez, a student counselor, went into another room and started grading. They took almost forty-five minutes examining my paper. When they opened the door, both men were shaking their heads.

Mr. Sanchez stared at me with a strange look on his face. "Same as before, a perfect score," he said.

Father Bayon wasn't surprised at all to hear the great news. I went to my mother and grasped her hands. Smiling brightly, I looked at Father Bayon.

"What's next?" I said.

Father Bayon looked over at Mr. Sanchez. "Can you find out about taking a college test?"

Mr. Sanchez studied me for several moments. "Ali, I will make a call to the college dean. We can get you the books that you will need. Now, this test will cover every subject the school has to offer. It will be just like the high school exam, but a lot more in-depth. Do you want to continue?"

I looked at everyone standing around me. "I do," I said.

"Well then, I will put works in motion and get the books. Father Bayon will have them delivered to you."

"Thanks. That would be wonderful. A lot more books that I can read! Yippee!"

Returning home in a padyak, all I wanted to do was go back to my job of sweeping the leaves in front of my mother's store. It wasn't a burdensome job, instead, it gave me pleasure to help my mother.

*****

Thursday morning of the following week, a delivery truck pulled up in front of our house. Father Bayon jumped out of the passenger side with eagerness and trepidation showing on his face.

"Hello Ali."

"Good day, Father," I said, reaching for the back of his hand and putting it to my forehead.

"Ali, Mr. Sanchez has sent over one-hundred-and-forty books. There are so many, it took a delivery truck to make this haul. How long do you think it will take to go through all of these?"

I looked at all of them. "Give me one week and I'll have them finished."

The truck driver loaded a group of boxes onto a hand truck and brought them into my room. After the last box was delivered, I thanked him.

Father Bayon looked at the pile of boxes sitting on my floor. "Let me know if you need more time studying all these books. There's no hurry."

"I will. I want to take the college test one week from Monday if that is okay with you."

"Are you sure?"

"I like the challenge of knowing that I have a deadline," I said.

Now I had the task of sorting all the books into different categories. There were languages, mathematics, sciences and history. I picked up a science book first, opened it up, and started reading. My mother walked into my room and nearly tripped over the pile on my floor.

"That's a lot of books," she said.

"It is," I agreed.

"Ali, what are you going to do with all this knowledge that you are receiving?"

"Not sure," I said, "but I hunger for more."

"Your father will be home tomorrow. I have spoken to him and he wants to see you very much. I'll leave you alone now so you can go back to your studying."

Once my mother left, I returned to my task. I didn't realize how much time had passed when my mother knocked on my door.

"Ali, it's time for bed," she said.

"Okay momma. I need five more minutes to finish all the science books. "After finishing my last page, I looked at the pile of unread books that laid before my feet. I'll finish the rest of you tomorrow," I said to the books.

*****

The next morning, there was knock on my door.

"Ali, its daddy." I set down a history book and jumped up to answer the door.

"Daddy, you're home!" I said, giving him a big hug and a kiss on his cheek. "I have missed you so much."

My father pulled back and looked at me with quizzical eyes. "Ali, I have been hearing some wonderful things about you. Your mother and I haven't the faintest idea on how you came about having this gift of knowledge." He gave me another hug and that's when he noticed all the books that were in my room. "How are you going to read all of these?"

"I have already finished those," I said, pointing to a pile that was gathering in a corner of my room."

"All of them?"

"Yes, they can be returned back to Father Bayon."

"How long have you had all of these books?"

"Since yesterday."

Your mother and I are totally speechless as to what is taking place, but you can count on us to be there for you, no matter what happens in the future," my father said.

"Thanks daddy. That means a lot to me."

As I became involved with my studies, I lost track of time. The shadows that occupied my walls everyday had left. Sunday night was upon me and I needed to get to sleep, but I couldn't. My mind was full of so many thoughts. I must have dozed off eventually because I awoke to a beautiful Monday morning sunlight streaming through my bedroom curtains. Lying there, I could see particles of dust floating in the air. As I watched the dust for several minutes, I knew the world was not going to stop for me. When I walked into the kitchen, my parents were putting the finishing touches on their breakfast. My mother glanced over the top of her coffee cup.

"Your father and I will be taking you to the school this morning. Sit down and eat. You will need all your energy to pass this test."

"Momma, what if I don't pass this test? What happens to me after?"

Picking up my father's dishes, she said, "Well I guess you will still go on living a normal life."

I finished my breakfast and headed to my room to get dressed. Looking at myself in my mirror, I felt a little nervous. After several moments, I convinced myself that I could do this. It was just like any other test that I have taken. Take several big breaths and move on with it.

*****

My parents and I arrived at the entrance of Zamora Memorial College at eight a.m. Father Bayon and Father Castillo, as well as the deans from every college and university in the Albay Province, were gathered in the administration office. It seemed Father Bayon had been spreading the word around town about me. All the students that I passed in the hallway gave me a high-five. A student faculty staff led me to a room similar to the previous exam rooms. Several university school administrators had been given the task of administering the college exam.

Dean Alverez stood next to me and explained, "This test will take approximately four hours. Once this door is shut, you cannot leave until you are finished. Do you understand?"

"I do."

"You can now begin," he said.

Everybody gathered around the administrators to talk about the exam. Mr. Alverez looked at the group of professionals and Ali's parents.

"The shortest time that any student has ever taken this test was two hours and forty-eight minutes. This particular student only scored a B," he told them.

When I circled my last answer and the test was completed, I felt confident, but I was really tired. Within thirty-eight minutes, I handed my test to Mr. Alverez.

"I'm finished. Mom, Dad, may we go home now?"

"You don't want to stay and see how you did?"

"No. I'll find out soon enough," I said as I grasped both my parents' hands. "Thank you for being here with me," I told them as I looked up at them.

My parents looked down at me as we walked away. My father squeezed my hand gently as he said, "We wouldn't have missed this for the world."

*****

Stopping just before we crossed the street to our little house, I could see the leaves had returned to their resting place in front of my mother's small store. Picking up my broom, I began sweeping. I noticed a peculiar looking leaf. I bent down and picked it up. Holding it to the sky, I noticed the different shape it had as I compared it to all the others. "Why are you different? What makes you so special?"

Minda, my best friend in the whole wide world, saw me sweeping. She ran toward me and sat down near my pile of leaves.

"What's up?" she asked. Minda and I shared our stories and thoughts about everything.

Sitting down next to her, I explained, "I just took a college test and didn't stay to find out if I passed."

Minda looked shocked. "Wow, a college exam? I have trouble with the first-grade test!" she said. I told her my secrets about taking the test. She gave me a high-five. We giggled and laughed loudly for a few minutes. I spent the rest of the afternoon playing with Minda and having fun. My mother had just finished preparing the evening meal when I heard her call out, "Time to eat." We said our goodbyes and I left to wash up.

"I saw you and Minda were having fun playing."

"We were," I said, smiling at my mother. Having dinner with my parents is something I truly enjoy since my father works out of town and I don't get to spend much time with him. Putting his dinner plate into the kitchen sink, he turned and faced me. "Ali, I have to leave tomorrow and head back to work."

"Okay, daddy." He came and sat down on the sofa next to me.

"Daddy, will you be here for me if I need you?"

"You know I will. You have your mother get in touch with me and I'll be here, no matter what."

"Thanks daddy," I said, reaching over to give him a big hug. There was a knock on our front door. My father got up to see who it was and I could hear him speaking.

"Hello Father Bayon, Father Castillo."

"Hello Francis."

My father's voice seemed excited as he asked, "How did Ali

do on the college exam?"

"That is why we came by. We wanted to tell her personally. Ali, you passed this test just like before." I smiled from ear to ear. "She possesses a knowledge that we cannot explain."

Father Castillo made the sign of the cross. "There are greater powers at work here that no human can understand."

"Francis, may we come in and talk with you and Christina?" Father Bayon asked. Everyone moved inside.

"After Mr. Alverez graded Ali's test, it left him speechless. He kept saying that no one has ever accomplished so much with so little to work with, and at an age of four. He went on to explain that he was contacting the President of the Philippines himself to inform him about Ali. We also discussed what would be in Ali's best interest." Father Bayon looked at the three of us when my mother walked into the room. "The Philippine government wants to send Ali to a school called, *The World Study of Interacting Students*. Only the brightest and smartest students from around the world can attend," he said.

My father took a sip from his coffee cup. "Where is this place located?"

"It's in Switzerland."

My mother looked over at my father. "We cannot afford to send her," she said.

"We understand. Everything will be paid for by the Philippine government."

My father raised his eyebrow. "Why would they do that?"

Father Castillo joined in on our conversation. "Because someone with Ali's gift can help our country and the world find new ways to feed the hungry, invent new things, or create jobs to help put people back on their feet. The possibilities are endless."

My mother's emotions were kicking in. "How long would Ali have to go to this school?"

Father Bayon opened an envelope. Studying it for several

moments, he said, "The schooling lasts for five years. When she finishes, she would be brought back here."

My father rubbed his face with his hands. "There's nothing here. She needs to be in a larger city," he said.

Father Castillo remarked, "She can go anywhere she would like."

I kept quiet, listening to the grown-ups discussing my future. My father knelt in front of me.

"Ali, Father Bayon was explaining about a school that only students like yourself can attend," he said.

My mother spoke with a raspy voice, "It's located in Switerland."

My father looked at me as though I was an adult and not a four-year-old child. When I looked back at him, I could tell that he was also having emotional thoughts.

"How long is this school?" I asked.

My father gazed into my eyes. "It will last for five years," he said.

"Do I get to come home?"

Father Bayon's voice was strong and positive as he explained, "No. They have very strict rules about leaving. You will be studying at very fast pace and there will be no time to stop."

"When does this school start?"

"It begins in January."

Looking back at my mother, I could tell that she did not like the tone of the conversation. I needed to know more things about this school.

"How many students attend this school?" I asked.

Father Castillo began to read the papers that came in the envelope. "At last count, there was twenty-four students. All the professors there are former students. Each student that completes the course must come back and teach there for two years after they have been in the field for at least five years. This way they bring new ideas and can relate to the new students."

"Ali, since you have passed the college test, you are being considered for this school. I was told that if you go there, you would be the youngest student to ever have studied there."

*****

The next morning, Father Bayon knocked on our front door. Opening my eyes to the beautiful sunlight pouring in my window, I yelled out to my mother, "What time is it?"

My mother, who was headed to see who was knocking, yelled back to me, "It is time for you to get out of bed."

"Is Ali here?"

My mother raised her voice, "Ali, Father Bayon is here to speak with you."

I walked into the front room with a bath towel in my hands. "Hello Father," I said, taking his right hand and pressing the back side against my forehead.

Father Bayon seemed excited. With shaking hands and an upbeat tone in his voice, he said, "Ali, I have some wonderful news. The mayor received a letter from the government in Manila and I was asked to deliver it to you. The only writing on the envelope reads: *To Ali*." My mother seemed shocked that I would be getting an official letter.

"Who is it from?" she asked. My hands were shaking as I opened the envelope. My heart was pounding heavily in my chest, as I read it and handed it to my mother.

Momma gasped, "Oh my! The president is coming here to meet with Ali."

"When?" The Father asked with excitement and jubilation in his voice. "It says he will be arriving on the sixteenth of November."

"That doesn't give us much time to prepare. I have to tell the mayor and let the church know."

I could tell the Father was very happy with this good news. "Ali, do you need anything?"

"Any books on science and mathematics would be wonderful."

"I'll see what I can do."

After Father Bayon left, I sat next to my parents on our sofa. "Mom, dad, I'm not sure about this school."

Both of my parents looked at me with admiration. My mother spoke softly, "We thought that this is what you wanted." I put my arms around her and held her tightly. With tears rolling down my cheeks, I looked into her eyes.

"Right now, I don't know what I want. I enjoy studying for these tests and all the attention that I have been getting, but to move away from you and daddy for five years? Well, that's a very long time."

My father's voice trembled as he spoke, "Indeed it is. Ali, you are now making life decisions that most young adults start to face. We wish that this did not happen to you, but some things are not explainable and this one tops the list."

My mother moved her hand slowly to mine. Picking up my hand, she held me gently. I could see that her emotions were getting to her.

She smiled at me. "A normal childhood is a wonderful thing in life. Growing up with friends and family, learning to ride a bike, falling, scraping your knees, playing dress up and make believe are what children do."

"I know momma. I would like to have these things as well, but I have this feeling inside that wants so much more. I see a book and I want to know what's in it. I hear stories about people being hurt because of typhoons and I feel sick to my stomach. I want to help people who are hurting. They didn't ask for these things to happen to them, but they did and now they are suffering because of it. No one should have to suffer so much and have so little. I want to make our world a better place."

My dad looked at me and said, "Ali, you have answered your own questions and I think that whatever you decide to do, you'll know that it will be the right choice. Your decision will be no small task, but after seeing for myself what you are capable of, I know you'll make a difference."

"Thanks for understanding me."

My dad walked over to me and gave me a big hug and a kiss on the forehead as he said, "I could not be prouder than I am right now."

- *Chapter Three* -

Mayor Thomas Manalo was just finishing up a conference call when Father Bayon entered his office.

"Good afternoon, Father," he said.

"Good afternoon, Thomas."

"Are you ready for some of the most fantastic news?" Thomas looked over the top of his glasses.

"The President of the Philippines is coming here in two weeks to visit one of our very own citizens," the Father said with excitement.

Thomas turned around, staring out his office window and rubbing his beard. He turned back to face the Father.

"The town of Bacacay, much less the province of Albay, has never had a president come here to speak to one of our citizens," he said.

"I know," Father Bayon said with excitement.

"What's this all about?"

"We have a small child named Ali Cruz that lives here with her parents and she is being considered by our government to be the smartest child ever to have lived in the Philippines."

"Say what?" The mayor asked with a raised eyebrow.

Father Bayon continued, "She is only four-years-old and has passed every test that has been given to her with a perfect score. A two hour test takes her less than thirty minutes to complete."

Contemplating the information for a moment, Thomas raised his right hand up to his face. "How is she doing this? Is she cheating?" he asked.

The Father replied, "She can read college books on any subject and answer any questions with perfect accuracy. President Datu has gotten word about her and wants to see her for himself."

Thomas thought for a moment. "We need to have the greatest test ever written to give to her and let the president see her take this exam," he concluded.

Thomas sat at his desk and called his secretary. "I want a conference call with the deans of the five best universities in the Philippines. Set up a meeting with them as soon as possible," he instructed. "We will hear something shortly. I will ask these deans to put together a test that no normal person would be able to pass," he said.

Father Bayon became concerned. "Does Ali get to study for such a test? She will need books pertaining to the subjects."

"I will ask the deans to send textbooks on all the subjects, but why does Ali need these books?" he asked. "I thought she knew everything."

The Father answered him, "If you have never studied anything, how are you going to answer the questions? You have to remember that she is only four-years-old."

"Will it take a long time for her to study for such an exam?"

"No. She can read a college book very quickly, answer any question out of it, and never miss an answer."

Thomas stood staring out the window. "Amazing," he muttered.

Father Bayon got up to leave the mayor's office. "I'm going over to see Ali," he said.

"Hold on for a moment," said the mayor. "Let me cancel my appointments for this afternoon. I would like to meet this young lady for myself."

The mayor's private car was waiting outside when he and Father Bayon exited city hall. The Father gave the driver the address to Ali's house.

*****

We heard a knock on the front door, and my mother looked out our picture window to see Father Bayon and another man standing there. She opened the door to let them in.

"Hello Christina, this is Mayor Manalo. He wants to meet with Ali. After I told him about the president coming, he asked to meet Ali for himself."

I was playing in the yard as I noticed my mother standing just inside the doorway talking to the two men. My mother walked to the back door of our home. "Ali, you have visitors," she said. "This is Mayor Manalo. He wanted to meet you in person." As I greeted them, I put the mayor's hand and then Father Bayon's hand against my forehead.

"Hello sir," I said.

The Mayor looked down at me and raised his eyebrows. "How old are you?"

"I'm four-years-old."

My mother explained to the mayor about when she was pregnant and some of the hardships she went through during her pregnancy. I left the room for a moment and brought back water for both men. Mayor Manalo studied me for several moments.

"Ali, I have asked five different universities to make a test that you will take when the president arrives. That way he can see for himself, how special you are. I have also asked that they send me books on every subject that will be covered in the test. They should be arriving here in a few days. We will be in touch with you once I hear from the president's personal secretary about his arrival and where the meeting will take place."

My mother and I thanked them for coming over with the news.

*****

As the mayor and the Father were entering the mayor's car, Mayor Manalo rested his arms on the car top. "Who would have ever known about this remarkable young girl?" Father Bayon looked over at him, "I can only think of one."

The mayor's office staff were scrambling for the next two weeks to make the president's visit a memorable one. The first call after meeting with Father Bayon was to call the governor's office.

"This is Mayor Manalo in Bacacay and I need to speak with Governor Mendoza immediately."

"Hold on for a moment."

The governor came on the line. "Hello Thomas, what can I do for you?"

"I just got word that the president is coming to see one of our citizens here in Bacacay," the mayor said with excitement.

"Why would he be coming here?" the governor asked.

"We have a small girl of four-years-old that has an intelligence far greater than anyone in our country."

The governor nearly dropped the phone in disbelief. "Come again?" he asked.

"She has passed every test from elementary to college exams with a perfect score. She can read a college book in minutes and know everything that is in it."

"But how?"

"We don't know how she's doing this, but it's happening, and the president has found out about her and wants to meet her here."

The governor looked at his appointment schedule. "When is all of this supposed to happen?"

Mayor Manalo replied, "In two weeks. The president will be here on the sixteenth of November at ten in the morning."

"Okay Thomas. Keep me in the loop of everything that's going on. I'll make some changes in my schedule. I do not want to be left out on any information."

Mayor Manalo called the president's secretary to discuss security issues and where the meeting would take place. After he hung up, a call was placed to the chief of police.

"The presidential meeting will be held at city hall. The auditorium will seat approximately one-hundred people. We are going to have five deans from the top universities joining this meeting as well as the press from all news channels. There will also be many governors from different provinces attending," the mayor explained.

The police chief thought for a moment. "That is a very tall order on such short notice," he said.

"Get with the president's security staff and find out what is needed for this meeting to take place."

*****

It didn't take long for the news to create a firestorm. Mayor Manalo's office was a hot bed of news. All the television channels began reporting on the historic meeting. This kind information also caught the attention of a small-time crook named Andres Salazar..

"She would bring a nice price on the open market," he said to himself. He shouted to his right-hand man, Marcos De Castro, "Check this out in Bacacay and find out all you can about this girl."

*****

My books had arrived just as the mayor said. A very large truck rolled up to my house and several crates were unloaded into my living room. The driver set the last box down.

"There are two-hundred and sixteen books in these boxes. Sign here please." I signed the papers and the driver left.

My mom just shook her head and said, "This task will be

monumental."

"Yah I know," I squealed happily.

I started dividing the books into categories: science, math, literature, history, languages and religion. After organizing all the books along my bedroom walls, I picked up the first book on the stack and began reading. Twenty minutes later, I closed the cover and put it on the floor. I then picked up book number two. Repeating this process, my mind wanted more data.

"Fifty-eight books and counting," I told myself. It brought me great pleasure tackling all the knowledge they contained. "Tomorrow I'll start early and should have a lot of these done."

The next morning, I hit the pile of unread books with determination. My eyes caught my mother standing at my door watching with amazement at how fast I was reading. My fingers were a blur. For several days, she would come in and watch me as I read.

One morning, she leaned against the door molding and whispered to herself, "My four-year-old, taking on the world like there is no tomorrow," then, she left the room to attend to a customer at her small store.

*****

"Hello Mrs. Diaz. What can I get for you today?"

"I just need a few things for dinner tonight. How is Ali?"

"She's fine."

"I heard on the news that the president is coming to see her."

"That's what we have heard."

"Everything is changing," said Mrs. Diaz. "You don't have the president come to visit just anybody."

"Nothing is changing. Ali is still here, and she still plays with the local children. She just has a special gift."

"That's what I mean, that special gift. It makes her different than all the other children. There is talk around the neighborhood that she is not like everyone else."

Ali's mother clenched her teeth. With a raised voice, she said, "She's not like anyone else and neither is your child or Mrs. Munio's children. Yes, she is different but that makes her special. And I wouldn't change her for anything in the world. Someday we will all look back at her gifted mind and admire how much she helped her country and family. Good day, Mrs. Diaz."

Mrs. Diaz set her basket down and walked away without buying anything.

*****

My mother was shaking when I approached her.

"What did Mrs. Diaz want?" I asked.

"Just spreading rumors. Typical of people who don't want to try to understand someone who may be different than them."

I walked over to my mother and gave her a hug. Momma looked at me with tears flowing from her eyes.

"Ali, I love you so much. I will not let anyone walk all over you just because you are different than the other children. It just burns me up to think that she has the audacity to talk about you like that."

"I love you too, momma."

- Chapter Four -

Father Bayon decided to check on Ali's progress with her mountain of books. Her mother saw him walking up to the front of her store.

"Hello Father," she said.

"Hello Christina. How is your day?"

"It's wonderful. And yours?"

"Never better," he said, but he noticed Christina's eyes were red from crying. "Did I interrupt something?" he asked.

She caught on to what he was referring to. "Oh no, I just had to deal with some gossiping neighbors."

"Well, how is Ali making out with all those books?" he asked, changing the subject.

"She has been hitting them hard. Would you like to see her?"

"Yes. I would."

Ali's mother closed the door on her store. "Let's go talk to her."

When Father Bayon entered the house, he couldn't believe how many books there were.

"Ali, where are you?" he called.

"I'm down here," I answered.

Working his way through the maze of stacked books, he discovered me sitting on the floor.

"I don't want to interrupt you, but I just wanted to get an update. The mayor and the church patrons were asking me questions and I didn't have any answers, so here I am."

I got up and put the Father's hand to my forehead.

"I just finished all the books."

"All of them?"

"Yes."

He knew not to ask any more questions about the books. "I'll let the mayor know," he said.

*****

Returning to City Hall, Father Bayon entered the mayor's office. "Thomas, Ali has finished all the books," he said immediately.

"All of them?"

"Yes. All."

"My, my. I didn't think she could pull such a task off. That was a lot of books."

The Father smiled brightly as he answered, "I know."

The mayor's tone changed. "Father, another problem has come to my attention. The police chief has just informed me about a shady character named Marcos De Castro. He has been asking some questions around town about Ali."

"What kind of questions?"

"All kinds. Where does she live? Does she go to school? Those kinds of questions."

The Father wrinkled his brow. "I see," said the Father with a worried looked on his face. He began rubbing his cross that he wore around his neck. "What do they want with Ali?"

"It's what she knows that they are interested in," replied Thomas. "She would bring a lot of money to a potential kidnapper. I have notified the police chief to look into this matter."

Father Bayon knew all too well about children being taken. "Ali looks like she could use some protection." he said.

Thomas picked up his phone and placed a call to the president informing him about the situation. After several minutes of speaking with him, Thomas hung up the phone.

"The president says that he will send a special person down that can handle the job," he told Father Bayon.

The Father looked hesitant. "And who would that be?"

Thomas looked out his window. "Her name is Neala Gonzales. She was born in Israel. Her father is Filipino and her mother is an Israeli. She was in the Mossad and did several tours in Iraq. She has dealt with these types of people before."

"Thomas, you know that I don't like to turn to violence. It has never gotten humans anything but grief. But I also know that there comes a time when such matters need to be dealt with and this is one of those times," Father Bayon said.

Thomas looked at the top of his desk. "I understand," he said with a nod.

Within an hour, Neala placed a call to the mayor's office and after a brief conversation, a place to meet was agreed upon. Neala didn't waste any time once she entered the mayor's office.

"Do you have the documents that I asked for? Where is Ali now?" she questioned.

The Father spoke up, "She should be home."

Neala stood in front of the mayor's window looking at the town. "These low-life crooks are probably watching Ali's house by now. They are waiting for the right time when Ali would be the most vulnerable to snatch. Go there and have her come to the church. I'll meet you there."

*****

Father Bayon came to my house and told my mother that he had a project at the church and that he could use my assistance. I was eager to be able to help.

Getting into a padyak, the Father turned to me, "Ali, I have been informed that you may be in danger. President Datu has sent someone that can help us in this matter. Her name is Neala. She used to work for the Mossad."

"Danger? What do you mean?"

"The mayor has received information about a criminal who plans to kidnap you and sell you to some other people. These people want to use your knowledge for ill-gotten gains. I'm not going to let that happen," Father Bayon said with a worried expression.

I felt overwhelmed and tears started running down my face. "Why would anybody want to hurt me?" I asked.

"It's because of the knowledge you carry in your head. Neala will be looking out for you and take any necessary precautions to keep you safe. Don't worry."

Father Bayon and I walked into the church and headed for the rear office. I saw a woman sitting in a pew with her head lowered as the Father and I walked by. She waited stealthily for almost five minutes. When she caught sight of a man walking briskly towards the church office, she quickly grabbed him along with the cell phone he was using. She silently took him out through a side entrance and ensured that he was no longer a problem. The person on the other end of the cell phone could still be heard shouting "Alonzo!"

Neala had a smirk on her face. "He can't come to the phone now," she replied smugly.

"Who is this?" the man on the phone asked.

"It's your worst nightmare," Neala said.

The police chief appeared from what seemed like nowhere and walked over to Neala.

"Is this the one?" he asked.

"The only one for now. He's just a scout. Take him back with you and find out what he knows. This problem has been resolved for now, but it will come again." Neala looked at us and said, "I need to leave for a little while, but I'll be back as soon as I can."

The Father looked up at Neala and said, "We'll be here for most of the afternoon."

*****

Neala headed to the police station to check on her capture. After a one and a half hour wait, she walked into police chief's office.

"Any luck?" she prompted.

"Not a word."

"Let me," she commanded. After a half hour, she had the information needed to solve the problem.

The chief looked at Neala. "How did you get it?"

"Lots of training in interrogation," she said.

*****

Neala sat in her car watching the house she had received information about. Not seeing any signs of activity, she shifted into first gear and moved forward in order to get a better view. Scanning the house from an obscure point, she caught sight of the sentry standing guard under an overhanging roof. Removing a shopping bag from her trunk, she grabbed a pair of sunglasses and a head scarf. She walked past a sentry that was smoking. As she turned the corner, she saw two more sentries walking the perimeter. Creeping slowly as to not draw attention, she made it to the next block. A call was placed to the police chief and she informed him of what she saw.

Two hours later, Neala constructed a plan to visit the person of interest. A little after midnight, a group of police officers and Neala began their assault on Andres Salazar's compound. Neala, dressed totally in black, moved like a ninja in the night.

With lightning fast motions, she took out two of his sentries in a matter of seconds. Two officers took out the other two with their stun-guns. Once she picked the lock, Neala had Andres on the floor before he knew what hit him. Cuffed, shackled and gagged, he wasn't going to make a scene. Marcus seemed to be sleeping in the next room when she entered his bedroom. He was not asleep, however. As he saw a dark shadow approaching, he suddenly jumped up from his bed, reaching for a gun that he kept on his bedside table. Before he could get to it, Neala shot him with a taser. After a few minutes of being incapacitated, he was taken out by several police officers

After removing the deadly force from the house, a complete search was needed to find out who was behind the operation. After digging through his books, Neala found out how he was going to take Ali and who his contacts were. Ali was to be sold by a person that the president would find quite interesting.

- *Chapter Five* -

Father Bayon was sitting across from the mayor when he received a call from the governor's office.

"What is happening with the president's arrival?" asked the governor.

"Well sir, the deans will be here on Wednesday and they want to set up a meeting with Ali. The president will arrive at ten on Thursday. His speech will take place at eleven and then Ali will take the test that has been prepared."

"Thank you, Thomas for keeping me up on the current events." Mayor Manalo hung up the phone and turned around in his chair to face the back wall. Staring at his diploma from the University of the Philippines, he stated, "This diploma took me many years of hard work and yet we have a young four-year-old girl in our community that has far exceeded that in such a short amount of time." The Mayor's phone rang again.

"This is Chavez, from the Emergency Management Office," said the voice.

"What can I do for you?"

"A super typhoon has just developed out in the Pacific, sir," Chavez replied. "Our early models indicate that it might head towards Legaspi City."

Thomas looked down at the floor and began to rub his face. "This can't be happening right now. We have the president coming here in a few days," he groaned. "What's our time-frame?"

Mr. Chavez's voice was sharp. "Four days tops," he said.

"Keep me posted," the mayor said.

Thomas looked across his desk at Father Bayon. Deep concern was evident on his face. He picked up the handset again, placing a call to the president's office. After several minutes, he hung up.

"Father, the president's staff still wants to have this meeting. A cancellation would put them back a considerable amount of time," he began. "Would you please inform everyone about the typhoon? We won't be able to have a big greeting for the president."

The following morning, the five deans arrived at Legaspi City Airport and were escorted over to the City Hall building in Bacacay. Dr. Bayani, from the University of the Philippines, noted to everyone present, "I have been put in charge of giving the exam to Ali."

"When can we meet her?" Dr. Alma asked with excitement.

Mayor Manalo looked at the deans sitting in his office. "Shortly," he said. "I would like to go with you, but I'm needed here since the typhoon is off our coastline."

All five deans looked at Mayor Manalo. They nodded in agreement. "We understand."

Father Bayon said, "I can escort the deans to Ali's home."

*****

My mother opened our front door and was surprised to see so many people waiting to meet me. She invited them in and came to retrieve me.

"Ali, Father Bayon is here to see you and he has brought some guests," she told me. I walked out to see a house full of people.

"Good afternoon Father," I said, taking his hand and placing it to my forehead.

Father Bayon smiled at me. "Ali, this is Dean Rommel, Dean Jose, Dean Romeo, Dean Alma and Dean Bayani," he said.

"Hello everyone," I replied. I took the back of each person's right hand and placed it to my forehead.

Dean Bayani stood in front of me. "Ali we just wanted to meet you and kind of test you a little bit, if you don't mind."

Suddenly, many questions were volleyed at me at once.

Father Bayon stepped in on the one-sided conversation. "One at a time, please. Nobody can answer them all at once."

They all apologized for the confusion. Each one took turns asking fairly difficult questions. I answered each question without hesitation and also noted that Dean Bayani's question should have been worded differently. "The answer for your question would not be correct," I said.

Dean Bayani thought a minute. "You are right. I have not thought of the question that way. By the way, good answer," said the dean.

The mayor's driver walked into the room. "We have to be getting back. The president's plane has just landed. The time table has been pushed up twenty-four hours due to the typhoon," he said.

Father Bayon turned to face me. "Ali, I will take the deans back to City Hall and have the driver come back to pick you and your mother up."

"Okay."

*****

My mother and I were standing outside our house when the mayor's car returned. As we entered the front of the building, my father was waiting by the door. My mother was shocked to see him.

"When did you get here?" she asked, kissing him.

"I was given a message from my boss and he put me on a company helicopter. He told me that it was too important to miss the President of the Philippines coming to meet my daughter. So, here I am," he said with a smile.

Moments later, everybody was led to the auditorium where they were seated. The exit doors were closed and covered by the secret service and the local police. President Datu entered the room and everyone stood up while he was escorted to the stage. Mayor

Manalo gave a short speech and introduced the president. A few moments later, I was asked to come to the stage, along with all the deans. They introduced me to President Datu and he shook my hand. I then placed his right hand to my forehead.

He began his speech, "Today is a great day for our beloved country. We are about to witness history in the making. A special test has been developed just for this occasion and I wanted to be present when this remarkable young lady takes such a test. She will have six hours to complete this exam. Ali, are you ready to take on the world?"

Looking up at the President, I answered, "I am sir."

They led me to another room and Dean Bayani was placed in charge of giving me the "Test of all tests!"

"Ali, you have six hours to take this exam. If you need anything, just ring this bell and someone will help. Good luck and Godspeed," Dean Bayani said and left the room. I opened up the booklet that was in front of me.

*****

The people in the auditorium were talking to the president, asking questions about anything and everything. Neala walked over and stood next to the president.

"Sir, I have some information that you need to be aware of," she said and quietly gave him the papers that were taken from Salazar's house. The president read a few pages.

"Where did this information come from?" he asked.

"I took them from someone who was planning to kidnap Ali, sir."

"I see. It seems that I have some dirty laundry."

Looking Neala straight into her eyes, the president said, "From one soldier to another, watch over her."

"I will sir."

*****

Mr. Chavez from Emergency Management came in the room with a worried look on his face.

"Mayor, we need to speak. Our window from the typhoon has been moved up considerably," he said with urgency.

Thomas spoke with an alarmed voice. "How much time do we have?"

"Eight hours," said Chavez.

The mayor stepped over to where the president was standing on the stage, "Mr. President, our time-frame for the typhoon has been moved up."

"How much time?"

"Eight hours before landfall."

The president nodded and said, "Keep me posted."

*****

I returned to the stage two hours and thirty-seven minutes later. Handing my exam to Dean Bayani, I said, "I think I spotted your particular question. It was like the one you asked me earlier."

"It was. I wanted to know just how intelligent you really are."

The other deans went to assess my exam papers. After an hour of grading the enormous test, they all agreed that I had aced it. No mistakes. No errors. President Datu came over and again, shook my hand congratulating me. I was filled with happiness as everyone in the room stood up and began clapping and cheering.

Someone began chanting my name and everyone in the auditorium followed, "Ali! Ali! Ali!"

The governors, mayors and deans walked over to me to shake my hand, one by one. My parents walked onto the stage with their eyes glinting. They were smiling brightly as they stood next to me.

I looked at them both with a big smile on my face.

President Datu took his place on my left side. Smiling, he shook my hand again as well as my parents' hands. The television cameras picked up on us as I stood there in the spotlight with the President of the Philippines.

"Ali, you will do great things. I wish I could stay longer and talk, but a typhoon is about to make landfall and I need to leave before it gets here."

"I understand. To be a president of a country takes a lot of time and being caught in a storm of this magnitude is something you cannot afford."

"Thanks for understanding. I will be in touch just as soon as the storm is over," he said.

- Chapter Six -

Typhoon Leizel began to make landfall along the upper Visayas Coastline. With wind gusts picking up considerably, President Datu had made his escape back to Manila. The police department sent out patrols telling everyone on a megaphone to head to the shelters. The chaos of so many people trying to make it to safety in time was horrible. Some of the elderly and special needs people had to be carried in or rolled in wheelchairs. Time was of the utmost essence and speed is a must in these situations.

Minda waived her arms and yelled to us in the crowd. We hugged each other as we moved towards the storm shelter. The wind began to howl, and the rain poured down upon the roof top with a heavy roar. The emergency power system flickered on.

With a dim, amber-colored light, everybody found a place to sit or lie down. We knew that typhoons can sometimes last for days at a time. Water bottles were passed out and Mayor Manalo began to speak.

"Everyone, please be quiet for a moment. We hope everybody made it here safely. If you know of anyone in your neighborhoods that need help, let us know so that we can get to them. As most of you know, President Datu was just here and came to see one of our own. Ali, would you please stand up for just a moment?"

I stood up next to my parents. The mayor raised his arms towards the group. "Everyone, this is Ali Cruz. She is only four-years-old and has just passed a university exam that would be almost impossible for just about anyone on the planet. She has aced this test as well as all the other tests that have been given to her."

A man leaning against a rear wall yelled out, "So, what does that mean?"

"We're not sure as of yet. The president wanted to come here and meet with Ali, but the typhoon has cut his visit short, and he said he would be in touch. Ali, would you like to speak to your neighbors and community?"

"Yes, I would. I don't know how I acquired this gift of knowledge or why. I thought I was like every other child my age, but that is not the case. I do not know what will happen to me, but I want to help in any way that I can with improving the lives of everyone here and in our beloved country. This is my home and I will not forget you."

Father Bayon spoke up, "I know where your gift came from. I have seen this with my very own eyes." The room fell silent. "In the coming years, Ali will expand her knowledge far greater than any human on this planet. God gave her this wonderful gift and he has a purpose for her. In time, she will show the world what she has in store for us."

Father Bayon led a prayer for the people and the township.

*****

For the next twelve hours, the typhoon pounded the Albay province. Word finally came from Emergency Management.

"Folks, the storm has now passed us by. You may leave now to go and check on your homes. The shelter will be left open for anyone who may need a place to stay," they told us.

Everyone stood up and walked around the room to where I was standing with my parents. One by one, they came to me and shook my hand or gave me a hug.

Father Bayon was the last in line. Hugging me tightly, he kissed the top of my head. Whispering softly, "My child, if you ever need anything, please let me know. I have many friends that can help you on your journey."

I looked up into his soft eyes. "I will Father."

*****

After we emerged from the shelter, we studied the city that laid before us. "It looks like our town was spared from a terrible ordeal," I observed.

Standing in front of our home, other than a few tree limbs in the yard and leaves that always appeared in front of my mother's shop, our home had not been damaged.

Many of our neighbors did not fare so well, however. Some had their roofs torn off or trees had fallen on them, making them unlivable.

Father Bayon turned and faced me. "Why do you think this happened?" he asked.

I studied the Father's face and I could not answer his question.

"Like I said, He has plans for you," Father Bayon said and walked away, heading for the church.

*****

Minda and her parents stopped at the front of our house.

"But how?" They murmured. "You didn't even lose a shingle on your roof. Ours has so much damage."

"I don't know why," my father stated. "This is how we found the place. You and your family are welcome to stay with us. I will help you in any way I can to repair your home."

People from around town had gotten word about my home and how it didn't have any damage from the typhoon. They began coming to see for themselves.

"How can this be? Ours looks like it has been through hell and their home has nothing wrong with it," one neighbor observed.

Father Bayon, during his Sunday service, was questioned about Ali's home and why she did not suffer like the rest of the community.

The Father stood in front of his congregation. Raising his arms, he said, "I cannot answer that question any better than you can. You all know about Ali's great gift, and I truly believe that mankind had no part in how she has acquired it. So, ask yourself why her home was spared from damage after such a typhoon." The congregation fell silent after that. They knew.

*****

Minda and I spent the next several days helping to clean up the mountains of debris around the neighborhood. Everyone was grateful for any extra help we offered.

My mother heard the front gate being opened. She looked out the window to see Father Bayon and Mayor Manalo coming up to the front door. She opened the door and invited them in.

"Hello Father. Hello Mayor."

"Hello Christina. Is Ali home?"

"She is." My mother turned to me and summoned me over to the door. Minda and I emerged from the hall.

"Ali, we just received a letter from President Datu. It's addressed to you. We wanted to bring it to you in person," said the Father.

"Thanks!" I said, as I eagerly opened it. It read:

"Dear Ali,

After returning to Manila, I was informed about the outcome of the storm and about how you have been helping your community. It would be my honor to invite you and your family to the presidential palace here in Manila. If you accept this invitation, please let my staff know as soon as possible. I'll be waiting to hear from you.
Sincerely,
President Datu"

I handed the letter to my mother.

"Oh my," she said. "A trip to Manila to see the president!"

Mayor Manalo put his hands in his pockets. "Ali, what do you want to do?" he asked.

"Sir, I am not sure," I said.

Turning to mother, I asked, "Momma, what do you think?"

"We need to talk with your father first. Then we can decide as a family what is best for you," she answered.

Using the mayor's cell phone, my mother placed an emergency call to my father's workplace. After a five minute wait, my mother told him about the possible trip being planned to Manila and the visit to the president. My mother was placed on hold again while he talked to his boss. When he returned, he explained that he was given a leave of absence. My mother hung up the phone.

"My husband will be home later tonight. We will discuss this trip and let you know tomorrow."

"That will be fine. I have been contacted with all the information concerning this trip. If you accept, then I will make the arrangements. You will need go the Legaspi City and pick out some new clothes."

My mother looked at the mayor and tilted her head. "How are we going to pay for that?" she asked.

"Everything will be taken care of by our government. My car will pick you up tomorrow morning at eight if you accept," the mayor explained with a smile.

"My father needs to know about this," I said.

"I will send a car to pick him up as well. He should be here in the next several hours," the mayor replied.

"Everything is moving at such a fast pace," my mother said overwhelmed with emotions.

"The president, he is a very busy man and his schedule is very demanding," explained the mayor.

*****

Just after six in the evening, my father walked into our house, and my mother and I rushed towards him and gave him a giant hug.

"I understand that a trip to the presidential palace is being planned," he said, raising an eyebrow. I gave him my letter.

"Now this is something that you don't get to see very often. Ali, would you like to visit the president at his palace?"

"I would daddy."

"Christina, what do you think?"

"Well it would be a trip of a lifetime. I don't see any problems," she said. After the family discussion, my father looked over at the mayor.

Mayor Manalo put his hands into his pockets. "Well, should I be here in the morning or tell the president you're not coming?" he said, chuckling.

Father Bayon spoke up, "I have also been asked to accompany you on the voyage, Ali, if that is okay with you and your parents."

Looking up at the Father, I said, "Of course." My parents agreed that it would be wonderful to have a friend and a priest come along.

"Neala has also been asked to accompany us," he added.

My dad turned toward the mayor. "Well I guess it's a go," he said with a nod.

"I will notify the president's staff about the arrangements and when to expect us to arrive in Manila."

Minda was grabbing my hand the whole time. "Wow! This is so exciting. Wait until I tell everyone in school tomorrow!" she exclaimed.

*****

Mayor Manalo's SUV was sitting in front of my house at eight in the morning. My parents and I walked to where he was standing next to the large vehicle.

"Ali, I have contacted the president's secretary and the arrangements have been made to get you to Manila. You will be leaving as soon as you pick out your new clothes. You and your parents will be staying in a very nice hotel. All expenses have been taken care of."

My dad grabbed my hand. "This adventure is going to be out of this world," he said. Looking up at him, I could tell that his head was already in the clouds.

On our way, I caught sight of my father staring out of the window at everything passing by. My mother watched him as well.

"A penny for your thoughts?" she asked.

He looked at her and just smiled. "This isn't happening, is it?" he mused. She leaned over and kissed him.

"It is, and this is our daughter."

The mayor instructed his driver to pull the car up in front of the Pacific Shopping Mall.

"Ali, there is a shop here that you may like. My grand-daughter shops there sometimes," the mayor explained. "Christina and Francis, there is a shop up that way that you may find to your liking," he said, pointing. "Give me a few minutes and I'll meet you there."

The mayor and I picked out some very fancy dresses and colorful outfits. Trying them on, I found that I loved the smell of new fabric. I felt like a queen as I looked in the mirror at each outfit.

After my bill was paid, we headed toward the clothing store where my parents went. They picked out a couple of nice outfits and the mayor paid their bill. The next shop was a shoe store. I tried on some really cool tennis shoes.

"Now this feels a lot different than the flip flops that I normally wear," I said.

Mayor Manalo saw me standing in front a mirror admiring the shoes I had on. "I don't think tennis shoes would be the appropriate attire for this visit. They are nice though," he said.

I put the shoes back on the shelf. Walking over to the dress shoe racks, I picked out a nice pair of shoes that would go rather well with the new clothes I chose.

As we walked out of the shoe store, the Mayor snuck back in and bought the tennis shoes I so admired. After paying for everyone's shoes, he gathered our group.

"Now to the airport. I have hotel arrangements made near the president's palace. You can get cleaned up and then head to the palace," the mayor said.

- *Chapter Seven* -

President Datu had a special turboprop plane that was used to take foreign officials around the country, waiting for us at Legaspi City Airport. Everyone knew that I have never been in an airplane before, and I was fascinated watching the islands drift by the windows as we flew over. The land mass looked like a jigsaw puzzle with all the different shapes, sizes and colors. I know that there are over seven-thousand islands here in the Philippines. Looking out each window in the plane, I got to see maybe fifty of them. As I stared, I wondered how many different dialects of the main language of Tagalog were spoken on all the different islands.

With my head leaning against the aircraft's fuselage, I could make out the coral reefs that surrounded the island's land mass. Boats of all shapes, sizes and colors were floating on the water. After an hour-and-a-half, the flight attendant announced that we would be landing in Manila shortly.

"Make sure your seatbelt is fastened securely as we start making our decent into..." she began, but our plane suddenly bounced as the wheels touched the tarmac. Loud noises erupted from the engines as the pilot adjusted the pitch of the propeller blades and threw the reverse thrusters in front of the exhaust to slow our speed.

After taxing for a while, our aircraft came to a spot on the tarmac away from all the other planes. We all breathed a sigh of relief.

*****

A limo pulled up alongside of us. The driver picked up our luggage from the cargo hold and loaded them into the trunk of the car. Climbing in the rear section of the limo, I feasted my eyes on the fine things that adorned the interior. There were flower vases, wine bottles, a television, and a private phone.

Looking out the side windows at the city that lay before me, I smiled brightly.

"There are so many people and the buildings are so tall. I remember reading about them, but I never dreamed that I would be seeing all these things," I said.

I could see that my parents were holding hands as we traveled about the city. It gave me great comfort knowing how much they loved each other. Watching me, they both smiled with admiration as I stared out the windows. The limo pulled up to the Manila Hotel and one of the president's personal staff met us once we arrived in front.

*****

"You are booked into several rooms. Father Bayon you'll be in Room 412. Neala, you are in Room 510, which is next to Ali's room. Ali, you and your parents are in the Presidential Suite," explained the woman, who seemed to be the president's secretary.

When the door to the suite was opened, I was amazed at how large the room was. I walked around the room, stopping at the huge window. I could see that the city was just starting to come alive with colorful lights. The sun began to set over Manila Bay. I was mesmerized by everything that I gazed upon. The presidential secretary watched us as we looked around our room.

"Mr. and Mrs. Cruz, you have this room and Ali, your room is through that door on the left," she said. Pushing the door open, I had a huge smile on my face. The room was enormous, far bigger than I'd ever dreamed of. It was decorated from top to bottom with beautiful décor that could have come right from a storybook.

"Do you like it?" she asked.

"Very much so," I replied in awe. "It's so beautiful here."

"President Datu chose this hotel. He thought that you may like it here."

"Thank him for me, please."

"I will. Dinner is at eight. Please be downstairs in the lobby no later than seven-thirty. Do be on time," she prompted.

I could tell just by looking and listening to this woman, her body language was a dead giveaway that she didn't like dealing with me and my parents. She watched me very closely as I made my way around the room with great admiration and looking at everything.

*****

Father Bayon and Neala were knocking on our door at seven-thirty. The Father looked at us.

"Is everyone ready? I'm starving," he said, smiling.

We made our way to the front of the hotel. The president's secretary watched as we exited the elevator.

"We have reservations for eight p.m. Let's hurry up please. We don't want to keep the staff waiting for our arrival," she said sharply.

After a ten minute ride, everybody scampered out of the limo. As soon as we entered the building, I noticed the Filipino décor on the walls. It was beautiful. I could see why we were going to dine here.

The secretary looked at our group. "I have chosen this restaurant because of its history. Many presidents from different countries have dined here."

The staff opened a private room for us. Once we were seated, I noticed that there were eight people on the wait staff. My parents watched me as I tried to take in everything that was happening.

"Our little girl," whispered my mother to my father. There was a tear on her cheek. Taking a napkin, he wiped it away.

"I think there will be a lot more surprises still to come. Some good and maybe some not so good too," he said.

I could tell by their facial expressions that everyone was enjoying their fine meal from this fabulous restaurant. The spices that were used in preparing our food were exquisite and delicious. The smells that emitted from the food as it was being served were wonderful.

The president's secretary prepared to give me instructions as she watched me enjoying my meal.

"Ali, you have a meeting with President Datu at three, tomorrow afternoon. Dinner will be at seven at the presidential palace," she said. "A car will be provided to take you anywhere you would like to go, and pick you up in front of your hotel for your visit with the president. Here is my number. Call me about anything that you may need," she said while she handed me a business card.

Studying her card, I said, "Thanks."

*****

After arriving back at the hotel, I crashed onto my bed and sank happily into the mattress. My mother walked into my room and kissed me good night. I settled in and the sound of soft voices drifted in. Even though the air conditioner was on, I could hear my parents outside on the balcony.

"Two days ago, I was sitting in front of our television with a fan blowing. Now I'm in a fine hotel with air conditioning," my father mused.

"I know," my mother replied. "Who would have ever thought that we would be here now? We will see what else is to come. I would have never thought that this would happen to us, but here we are. Our Ali," my mother sighed.

My father's voice was raspy as he wondered, "What has God got in store for her and for us?"

My mother squeezed his hand. "I don't think even Father Bayon can answer that one."

- Chapter Eight -

I was looking out my bedroom window as the sun began to rise over the horizon. I ran out of my room and crawled into my parent's bed.

"Momma, have you and Daddy ever been here in Manila?"

"We have," my mother said. "We were married here."

"You were? I thought that you two were married in Bacacay."

"No," my father replied. "My parents, your grandparents, were from there. Your mother is from Quezon City."

"So, how did you two meet?"

"I was working a construction job on a high-rise apartment building and your mother was working at the Mall of Asia. I just happened to go there to do some shopping and I accidentally ran into her. She belted a few words at me for being so clumsy and I did the same. After several weeks of going back to try to find her again, she was nowhere to be found. I was eating lunch at the Ocean Front Café, and low and behold! Your mother was a waitress there. I got up from my chair and ran into her again, knocking the dirty plates that she was carrying out of her hand."

"That's how we met."

"We were married on Manila Bay at sunset and the next year you came into our lives. Now we are three."

There was a sudden knock on the front door. My father looked over at us.

"Who is it?" he called out.

"Room service," said the voice at the door. I opened the door to a white-clad waiter rolling in a breakfast cart.

Moving closer to the cart, I said, "It smells so delicious."

Minutes later there was another knock on our door. I opened

the door to Father Bayon and Neala. The Father saw the food on the cart. "Don't eat just yet. Prayer Service!" he said. I gave him a funny look. "Just because I am not in a church, does not mean that I cannot pray. I am still a Catholic Priest."

"You are right Father. Where are my manners?" He gave a morning prayer on our balcony with the sunlight shining all its glory upon the earth.

Neala took a sip of her coffee. "After breakfast, we will go to the Mall of Asia. Ali, you can walk around and do some shopping if you like," she said.

I looked at our group. "I would like to find something for Minda," I said.

Neala and Father Bayon got up to leave. Neala turned to us and said, "The car will be here in an hour. Be ready downstairs."

*****

I was amazed at the sight of the Mall of Asia. It would take hours just to see all the stores. I found a small shop that had an array of necklaces.

"I think she'll like this one," I said, holding it up to the light. Neala's smile dropped and she suddenly looked uneasy.

Father Bayon saw her looking around and asked, "Is everything okay?"

"Not sure, just a feeling I have," she whispered.

Father Bayon paid for the necklace. "It's time to go back to the hotel and prepare for this afternoons meeting," he said. Everyone started walking back when I saw the *Ocean Front Café* sign.

"Is this the place where it happened?" I asked excitedly while running towards the entrance of the café. "Daddy, where were you sitting when you and momma ran into each other?"

My father pointed towards a table in the rear of the café. "I was sitting in that chair, by the railing overlooking the bay," he said. I walked over to the table, where a young couple was sitting, enjoying their meal. I smiled brightly at them. "Excuse me," I began, "I just wanted to see where my mother and father met. He was sitting where you are and she was over here." I pointed.

They looked at each other and smiled. "We met here too!" said the girl. "This is our favorite spot."

"Thanks for letting me stand here with you for a moment," I said bashfully. "Sorry for interrupting you."

"No problem. Our pleasure."

As I returned to the front of the restaurant, my father reached for my hand. "Ready to go?" he asked.

"Yes. I just wanted to…"

"We know," my mother replied before I could finish. "We know."

On the way back to the hotel, Neala spotted something wrong.

"Driver keep going straight," she said. He did as he was told. "Take a left turn here."

"What's going on?" my father asked.

"We are being tailed."

Neala placed a call to the president's security staff. "We are being tailed by a white Toyota sedan with License Number BMJ 845."

"Where are you now?"

"We just turned onto Nino Boulevard."

"Okay, I'll have some people there shortly. Do not stop," said the voice on the phone. Ten minutes later a black sedan saw our limo go through an intersection and watched for the tail. It only took seconds for the tail to be spotted.

Two more black sedans pulled in behind the white Toyota, with their lights flashing. You could hear tires squealing, as a third car pulled in front. Moments later, a hectic scene unfolded. With guns drawn, the two suspects were thrown down onto the hard pavement and were handcuffed.

"What's going on?" my mother asked.

Neala's voice was intense as she explained, "Ali has attracted some unsavory characters."

My father's voice raised up several octaves. "What do you mean?"

"There are kidnappers trying to take Ali," Neala said.

"What?" my mother shouted, with tears gathering in her eyes and a lump in her throat.

"Why am I just now hearing about this?" she demanded.

"Because we were trying to keep a lid on it, so we did not attract more bad people."

My father became upset. "It looks like you have a leak," he growled.

Neala responded, "It does seem so, doesn't it?"

"Neala, just who are you and how did you become involved with Ali?" my father asked.

"Mayor Manalo called President Datu. I was sent to watch Ali. The president knew that a young girl with her knowledge would likely attract bad people who'd want to take her. I found out that a person of interest was looking into kidnapping Ali. They were going to sell her to someone else that would use her knowledge to aid in their own criminal operations. That problem has been taken care of," she said.

*****

As we pulled into the hotel's parking lot, Father Bayon said urgently, "There are only a few hours left before Ali's meeting with President Datu. I'll meet you in the lobby at two forty-five."

Everyone rushed off to prepare for the very important meeting in the safety of our rooms, still shaken. Standing at the door of our hotel room, my parents were speaking quietly to one another. My mother spoke in a low voice, "Is this some of the bad that you talked about earlier?" she asked my father.

My father held her hand and looked in my direction. "It is and it's not going away," he answered.

A tear ran down my mother's cheek. "I don't like this one bit. Somebody wants to hurt my little girl."

Neala heard them as she walked towards her room. As she passed by, she whispered to them, "Not on my watch."

At exactly two-forty-five everyone was down in the lobby when the president's personal car arrived.

The same secretary got out and stood next to it as everyone climbed in. She spoke to the driver, "Let's go."

Fifteen minutes later, we arrived at the Presidential Palace. The car stopped at the guard shack and examined our papers.

As we reached the palace, I became mesmerized at the size of it. I looked at my parents in awe.

"Oh my," I said as we were led to a front chamber. The president's secretary stopped us from going any further.

"Wait here," she said and disappeared. A few minutes later, President Datu arrived and welcomed everyone to his home.

I was smiling as the president stood before us. "This is such a lovely palace," I said, marveling at the building.

"My wife says it too large for just the two of us. Our son is off to the university and does not live here," President Datu explained. "The main reason I asked you to come here, was to get to know you a little better, and to find out just what your plans are with your special gift."

The First Lady came into the room. "Ali, this is my wife, Rosanna," said President Datu. Following her was the president's secretary. "And you have already met my secretary, Mrs. Rolado."

"Yes, we met," I said.

Rosanna looked down at me. "Ali, just how old are you?" she asked with curiosity.

"I'm four-years-old."

"My gracious," she said. "My husband told me about you, but I wanted to meet you for myself."

President Datu asked, "Ali, have you thought about the school that Father Bayon spoke to you about?"

"Do you mean the *World Study of Interacting Students*?"

"Yes, that's the one."

"I have thought about it and I have decided to go," I told him.

"Wonderful."

Mrs. Rolado seemed confused. "What school is that?" she questioned.

"It's a special school for extremely bright individuals. There are no entrance exams to take and the only students that can attend are sponsored by their government," replied the president.

"Ali has a gift so rare that only a few people on this planet possess it. I have seen it with my own eyes."

"Ali, would you give us a small example of your special gift?"

"What would you like to know?" I asked.

"I have a book in my library that I would like for you to read and tell me about it."

"Okay, I will take a look at it."

Someone retrieved the book and placed it in my hands. I opened it and saw that it was written in Spanish. I studied every page, closing the book in around thirteen minutes. "Interesting book," I concluded.

The president studied my reactions. "Did you understand what you read?"

"I understood it completely. When the Philippines were under Spanish rule, Miguel Lopez De Legaspi was believed to have placed a Spanish treasure somewhere in the Albay province, but it was never found."

"That's correct."

"The reason it was never found is because they are looking in the wrong area."

The president's voice became high. "What?"

"They need to be looking into Leyte Gulf. Find the coordinates for the Japanese Battleship Musashi that sunk during the Second World War and then look north one kilometer," I explained. "There, a Spanish vessel named the Galvez was also sunk and that is where you'll find what you are looking for."

The president was shocked. "I'll have to check that out," he said at last. "Ali, I have asked the Dean over at the University of the Philippines, Dr. Bayani, to let you sit in on a science class for tomorrow. I think the school would like to see what a person of your knowledge could do in a real world classroom. I believe you met her when you took your college test."

President Datu looked around the dining table at all the people that sat with him. "Father Bayon would you say the blessing?"

"I would love to," he replied.

Afterwards, President Datu asked, "Father, what's your take on all of this?"

"I have asked everyone I know. No one can give me an answer. We all agree though there is a higher power at work here and we need not interfere," Father Bayon replied.

The president was wiping his mouth with his napkin. "I truly believe you are correct in your assumption."

Turning in his chair, he looked directly at me. "I will have all the arrangements made for you to attend the school. A plane will be at Legaspi Airport to pick you up on January the ninth at eight in the morning. Everything you will need will be attended to. I would like to see you when you return. I may not be the president when you get back, but I will find you."

*****

Everyone sitting at our table got up to return to the presidential office. Neala asked the president about security precautions. President Datu retrieved a notepad from a side desk, made a note, and handed it to Neala.

"Carry this with you always and you'll never have a problem," he said.

Neala looked at the note. It read:

"Neala Gonzales has been authorized by me, President Datu, to carry a weapon on her person at all times."

At the bottom of the note, was the President Datu's signature. She put the note away and President Datu made a call to his head of security.

*****

The next morning, we had to be at the University of the Philippines by seven-thirty a.m. Upon entering the main building on campus, a male student was waiting for us as we arrived. He saw four adults and one child walking towards him.

"Hello. My name is Milo Rolado. I have been asked to walk you to the chemistry class this morning."

Milo led us down a long hallway toward a very large classroom. I felt like I was in a zoo. Every student was staring and whispering. Our assistant went over and talked to the teacher. Moments later, the teacher, a Mr. Pascal, looked at me and then turned towards the class.

"We have a celebrity among us today. Her name is Ali Cruz and she is four-years-old." A murmur rose from the student body.

Someone spoke up, "What makes her a celebrity?"

"It seems that she has read every book that our university has. Ali, please come up to the head of the class. Can you solve the equation that I have written on the blackboard?"

I turned and looked at the problem. "May I?"

Mr. Pascal handed me the chalk. I found a small step stool so I could reach where he had written the problem down. Everybody started laughing. I wrote the answer in about fifteen seconds. Mr. Pascal smirked and came over to where I was standing. He looked at my answer and his expression was priceless. Stuttering, he turned towards the class, "Her answer is correct." I then turned and wrote out an equation for Mr. Pascal to work on. After studying the problem, he didn't know the answer. I saw Mr. Milo scratching his head as well. I could see the whole class jotting down everything that I had written on the board.

$$*****$$

On our drive to the airport my father asked, "What was that equation you put on the blackboard?"

"It was nothing, just a bunch of junk I put together that will take them days to try to figure out." Everyone began laughing.

Neala gave me a high-five. "You go girl," she said with a smile.

The noise from the aircraft was mesmerizing. I looked over at Father Bayon. He was silent and said nothing. My parents were having a very quiet conversation and Neala kept watching for anything and everything about the cabin of the aircraft. I sat next to a window watching the lights from the small towns and communities twinkle off in the distance. Neala placed a call to Mayor Manalo notifying him of our return. By the time we made it to our house, I was asleep. My father picked me up and carried me to my bedroom. My mother tucked me in and my parents stood by my door watching me for the longest time. Smiling, they turned off the light and shut the door.

- Chapter Nine -

Christmas Day has arrived and I knew it wouldn't be much longer before I would have to leave. It was a sad thought, knowing that my parents would not be there on my next five birthdays and Christmases. Hearing a knock on our front door, I opened it to find Father Bayon standing there with a small gift for me.

"It isn't much, but I think you may enjoy it," he said. I opened the present and there was a small locket with writing inside. It read:

"Be safe and keep him in your heart wherever you go."

I didn't know what to say. A tear began to run down my face. "Thank you, Father."

I noticed a bag that he had in his left hand. It seemed to be a little heavy. He saw me staring at it. Reaching in, he retrieved a large box.

"This is from Mayor Manalo," he said.

"What's in it?"

"Open it and see."

I tore into the box and there lay the tennis shoes that I had tried on in the mall. "Oh My!" I said with excitement and sat down to put on my fine new shoes.

Minda was standing near her house talking with another neighbor when she saw Father Bayon arriving at my home. She hustled over to my door and gave it a heavy knock. When I opened it, she immediately noticed my new shoes.

"I like your shoes! I also have something special for you," said Minda.

"And I have something for you," I replied.

Minda handed me a brown box. Inside it, there was a small,

beautiful wooden jewelry box.

"I made it myself," Minda said, smiling.

I began to sob. Between tears, I uttered, "It's beautiful. I'll treasure this forever."

I handed her my present and she whispered, "Thank you." Carefully opening the long, slender box, she removed the necklace. We both cried.

Father Bayon walked over to where we were standing. "My, my, what's with all the tears?" he asked.

Minda answered, "We are not sad. We are very happy."

The Father smiled at us. "Well now, that's the spirit."

My mother heard all the commotion. "What's going on here?" she asked, confused.

"The girls just exchanged presents and they are happy," answered Father Bayon.

"I see," my mother said with a large smile. "Father, would you like to share a Christmas dinner with us?"

"I would be delighted to."

"Father, may I borrow your cell phone to call Neala."

"Neala, its Ali. Would you like to join my parents, Father Bayon and myself for a Christmas dinner?"

"I would love to have dinner with you. What time?"

"Any time from right now."

"I'll be there shortly," Neala said.

"Okay," I said and hung up.

"Momma, Neala will be joining us."

My mother looked at Minda. "Are your parents' home?" she asked.

"They are."

"Can you ask them if they would like to join us for a Christmas dinner?"

A few minutes later, I heard a light knock on the front door through the all the chatter. As I opened the door, Neala greeted me with a big smile.

"Merry Christmas Neala," I told her.

"Merry Christmas Ali." I stood there blocking the door entrance unknowingly for several seconds. "May I come in?" she asked with a chuckle.

"Oh my! Where are my manners? Please do."

Neala scanned the group. "Merry Christmas everyone," she announced.

Moments later, Minda's parents knocked on the door. Minda looked through our front window. "My parents are here."

My mother pointed a finger at everyone. Counting heads, she realized she needed to add a few more chairs so that everyone would be able to sit at the table.

"May I say the blessing?" asked Father Bayon.

My mother looked at him. "Father, that would be wonderful."

The meal my mother prepared was wonderful. The smell coming from the kitchen was exquisite. She had prepared our favorite filipino dishes and my favorite desert, Flan. Sharing that moment with my family and friends would always be one of my favorite memories.

*****

I packed everything I own and placed it by the front door. Neala knocked twice, then opened the front door. Sticking her head in, she asked, "Are you ready?"

"I am," I said. She picked up my bags and took them to the SUV. My parents, Minda and I got in and we headed off to Legaspi City Airport. Sitting away from the other planes, sat a private jet, waiting for our arrival.

"Do we have to go through customs?" my mother asked.

Neala, just stated, "No."

My parents looked at each other and my father just shrugged his shoulders.

Minda was the first person to climb out of the van. I saw her staring up at the aircraft that stood before us. "How on earth does this thing fly?" she asked.

Watching her for a brief moment, I said, "I will teach you, in a few years." We both giggled.

The flight crew took our luggage from Neala and the van driver.

Standing at the entrance gate, Father Bayon was waving at us and started running onto the tarmac. Several police officers surrounded him as if he were a terrorist trying to take over the plane. Neala ran over to where they had him confined. Showing the officers her ID, she explained that he was with us. Walking away with Neala, he murmured, "I thought I was under arrest."

"You were about to be."

"Thanks for helping me," Father Bayon said.

"You're welcome Father."

"Would everyone gather around? I would like to say a prayer."

I hugged my parents and Father Bayon, thanking him for being there for us. My parents were a sobbing mess. I didn't want to leave them, but I knew that this was my destiny. I kept repeating, "I'll be coming back."

My mother was sobbing. "We hope so," she said. "Your room will be as you left it."

My father was choked up as well. "Neala, you watch over my little girl."

"I will. I'll guard her with my life," she said.

My father shook Neala's hand. "I know you will."

*****

President Datu had made special arrangements for Neala to

travel with me. Even though she was a secret agent, carrying a weapon was strictly forbidden at this school. I knew that Neala did not need a firearm to protect me. She was a master in all the martial arts.

Father Bayon took my hand and put something small in it. I opened my hand to see a little cross. "Add it to the locket," he said. Removing the chain from around my neck, I added the cross.

"May I?" he asked, returning it to its original location. "I'll be waiting to see you when you return."

With tears pouring down my face, I said, "Thank you Father."

Minda was wiping her eyes. "Take care," I told her, holding her hands. "I will never forget you." I wiped away the tears from my own eyes. Then, I hugged her tight.

She looked at me and said, "You better not."

Neala stepped over to us. "We have to be going," she said.

My parents knelt in front of me. I gave them both a big hug and kissed them goodbye. My mother's face was distraught. "Momma, I will be coming back," I reassured her and hugged her again.

Neala touched my shoulder. "We have to board now."

Once the door was shut, the airport security made everyone leave the tarmac.

Looking out a window, I watched my family and friends walk away. Our plane received clearance from the control tower and in a matter of minutes we were airborne. The flight attendant stopped to talk to us.

"We will be making a stop in Dubai for refueling," she said.

Neala studied the attendant. "Will we be getting off the plane?"

The attendant looked at her with curious eyes. "No, why?"

"I have an Israeli passport."

"I see. I'll tell the captain."

I looked up at the attendant. "Will there be anybody else coming with us?"

"Not that I'm aware of."

"Such a large plane for just the two of us," I observed.

"These larger aircraft can fly for longer periods of time," she responded.

After several hours of just sitting, Neala changed seats, moving closer to me. "Ali, when we are settled at our new location, you need to learn how to protect yourself," she said.

"Why?" I asked. "I'll have you there with me."

"Because I cannot be with you twenty-four hours a day. You need to know what to do if a situation comes up."

I looked straight into her eyes. "I hate violence."

"I do too, but there are people in this world that think differently and will not hesitate to do whatever it takes to get what they want. And that means, hurting people."

I nodded. I knew what she meant. We had already experienced some of the danger she referred to.

Standing up in the aisle, I said, "This flight to Dubai is going to take approximately seven hours and thirty minutes. Can I do cartwheels in the cabin?"

Neala gave a stern, "No," and added, "but I understand about the tired leg syndrome."

"I read every manual or magazine that I could find on this aircraft, except for the aircraft service manuals," I sighed.

I walked up to where the flight attendant was sitting. "Are there any manuals in the cockpit that I might be able to read?"

"I will check." Moments later, she returned with several large volumes of books. "Will this keep you busy for the rest of the trip?"

"No. I'll have these done before we land in Dubai," I answered. She gave a queer look and walked off.

Neala just watched as I read the service and flight manuals.

Looking over at Neala, I announced, "Now I know how to operate this aircraft!"

"I can see why some people want to take you. Your reading

speed is extraordinary."

The flight attendant came towards me. "Would you like something to drink?" she asked.

"Just water."

"Here are the aircraft manuals. You can return them now," I said, handing the books back to her.

"You finished all of these?"

"Why, yes."

"I will be serving lunch now. We have baked chicken and blackened fish, served with rice and mixed vegetables." Neala and I both chose the chicken. After the meal was served, I noticed Neala had begun to act suspicious.

"What's wrong?"

She responded, "Quiet."

"Excuse me," I replied. She gave me a stern look. Getting up, she headed towards the cockpit door. Neala caught a low conversation between the flight attendant and the co-pilot.

"Did the captain eat the fish?"

"Yes. Give him another ten minutes and he'll be out."

"I'll take care of our two passengers."

Neala told me to stay put, gave me a nod, and slipped into the restroom and shut the door. The flight attendant came over to where I was sitting. "Where's the other person?" she asked.

"I don't know. I was dozing off."

Neala came up behind the attendant and put her into a sleep hold. A few moments later, she was out. Neala put her finger to her mouth. Searching the flight attendant's pockets, Neala found a small pistol. Removing the gun, she tied and gagged the attendant so she would not be any more trouble.

Neala knocked on the cockpit door.

"Trouble," was all she said, in a low voice. The door opened and she pointed the pistol at the co-pilot.

"Out."

"Who will fly the plane?" asked the co-pilot, with panic.

Neala went into her commando mode. "Not your concern," she said.

Leaping out of the co-pilot's chair, he lunged at her, grabbing for the pistol. With cat-like reflexes, she hit him so quickly that he never even saw her right fist as she made contact with his chin. He crumbled like a wet rag hitting the floor.

Watching Neala implementing her training, I smiled at her. "A bad mistake on his part." He was no longer a problem. Tied and gagged, Neala put him in a closet.

"Ali, can you fly this aircraft?" she asked.

"I know how it works, but I can't even reach the rudder petals," I said. Thinking quickly, Neala removed the captain from the captain's chair and set him in a passenger seat.

"What happened to him?" I asked.

"He's been drugged. Probably from the fish. I think our flight attendant and co-pilot had other intentions for us. Sit in the co-pilot's seat and let's see if we can land this plane somewhere and not get ourselves killed. Ali, check and see if you can determine where we are at," Neala said.

Examining the GPS, I concluded, "We are headed towards Syria." Neala responded, "That's not good. Look at the pilot's maps, see if you can pick a place that we can put this plane down."

I studied the fuel gauges. "With the amount of fuel that we have left, we can probably make it to Sri-Lanka."

"Sounds good. Can you put the new coordinates into the GPS?"

"Done," I said. Our plane started to make a course change from the auto-pilot controls.

Neala was studying everything that lay before her. "Now, we have to radio for some help," she said. "Can you find the radio frequency settings for Sri-Lanka?"

I started looking for the co-pilot's radio book. Locating what I needed, I made the radio changes. After several attempts, I was able to make contact. I explained that our aircraft had been high jacked and we had retaken control. Emergency measures were put into place. Holding the earmuffs tightly against my head with my shaking hands, I relayed the landing coordinates to Neala. With the auto-pilot set, she released the steering controls. Searching the cockpit, she located a SAT-phone and placed a call to President Datu's office. As soon as he answered his private phone, he could tell that something was wrong. Neala explained what happened and that we were in serious danger.

"Are you okay?" the president asked with panic.

"We are for now, but I have never flown a jet before."

"I'll make a call to the President of Sri-Lanka and see if he can help you. How much time before you enter their air space?"

"About thirty minutes," Neala replied.

"I'll be in touch." A few minutes went by before the SAT phone rang. It was President Datu. "Neala, I have contacted President Silva and he is sending military personnel and police to the airport to assist you. Keep me informed after you land."

Neala hung up and placed a call to the tower.

"Aircraft N90215, this is Sri-Lanka Tower. What is your position?"

"We are approximately eighteen miles out."

"Start your descent to five-thousand feet on heading three-hundred-forty degrees. We have a north wind at twelve knots. I need you to start a turn to the north in one minute."

Neala responded, "Roger." There was a knock on the cabin door. "Ali, see who that is. I hope it's the captain." I opened the door slowly and Neala looked over her shoulder to see the captain standing there with sweat running down his face.

"What happened?" he asked.

"The flight attendant and the co-pilot were trying to take control of the aircraft. Right now, we are about to land in Sri-Lanka."

The captain was a little slow processing what had happened but seemed relieved that we had control of the situation.

"I'm talking to the control tower and they have emergency preparations on the way," Neala informed him. The captain nodded and made some gestures, indicating he was about to throw up. I left the cabin to retrieve a bag and a bottle of water for him.

"Here, Captain."

"Thanks," he said, taking a long drink of water.

"I have never flown a plane, much less a jet," Neala said.

The captain made a few more groaning noises. "What's our altitude?" he asked.

"We are at twelve-thousand feet."

"Take us down to five-thousand feet," he said.

"Flight N90215, this is Sri-Lanka Tower, make a left turn in five seconds." The captain put on the co-pilot's headphones.

"Sri-Lanka Tower, this is Captain Fargo of Flight 90215. I was drugged, but now I'm now back in the cockpit."

"Okay good Flight 90215. Make a left turn now and descend to five-hundred feet. You should be able to see the runway."

The captain responded, "I see it." He tried to pull the lever for the landing gear. His hands were shaking terribly as he gripped the steering wheel.

"May I?" I asked, pulling the lever. With a gargled voice, he thanked me.

- Chapter Ten -

Our aircraft was returned to service after a maintenance crew refueled it and all the food and beverages were replaced. A new flight crew was brought in and Neala went through all of their flight books to check for any problems. After checking and rechecking, she was finally convinced.

"Everything is okay," she said to me as I boarded the plane.

I studied Neala's face as she watched everyone that had anything to do with the aircraft. We couldn't take any chances. With everything prepared, we were off again. I could tell that Neala was a little on edge and didn't want to let her guard down. One attempt was enough. Once we were airborne, I re-read all the books that were on board and then I got bored.

"Neala, is there anything else that I haven't read or done yet?" I asked.

"Do you play chess?" she suggested.

"I never have, but I would like to learn."

Neala got out her tablet and brought up a chessboard. She explained the rules and how to play the game.

She explained, "Chess is a very mental game and requires a great deal of thought."

I liked the sound of it already. We played for almost six hours and I was up eight to one. I had to let her win some or she might not want to play anymore.

*****

Our flight time to Zurich, Switzerland was another eight hours. Boredom took its toll and I fell asleep. I did not awaken until I heard the wheels making the landing noise as we touched down.

Staring out the windows, I could see a white blanket covering everything. Neala noticed what I was looking at.

"I hope you brought some warm clothing," she said.

"Why?"

"That is snow."

I looked back to the white blanket. "I have never seen snow before," I said with amazement.

"It's cold and not very pleasant," said Neala.

"I don't have clothes or a coat to deal with this kind of weather."

"We will have to go and buy something. I don't have the proper clothing either," she said.

A limo pulled up to our aircraft. I made a mad dash, diving into the backseat to escape the cold. I had never had to ride in a car with the heater on, but I was glad to feel the warm air. Neala stepped in and closed the door. I looked at her.

"Now that is cold air!" I said.

Once our luggage was placed into the trunk, we were off to the customs office to be cleared. Afterwards, a shopping trip was in order. The town looked just like a Swiss postcard. Small shops, a bakery, a few restaurants for the tourists, and several clothing stores lined the street. Warm clothes were at the top of my list.

Looking at Neala, I said, "This kind of weather is going to take some time to get used to."

Neala responded to my comment, "It does indeed."

After purchasing some warmer clothing, we were off to our new home for the next five years.

*****

It took another half hour of travel before we pulled onto the last road that would take us to our new home.

Topping a rise in the landscape, I could see down in the rolling valley, a very large castle.

"Is this where we will be staying?" I asked.

The driver looked over his shoulder. "Yes it is. That is Rorris Castle."

"How old is it?"

"It was built in sixteen-forty-eight," he said.

Our car pulled up to the front of the castle and stopped in front of a small group of people who were standing along the steps of the driveway. A tall man with gray hair stepped forward to greet us. "Welcome to Rorris Castle. My name is Roger Whitaker. I am the Headmaster of the World Study of Interacting Students. You'll be shown to your rooms and lunch will be served in thirty minutes in the main dining room. Your luggage will be brought up to your rooms momentarily," he said.

Just inside the main entrance of the castle, I noticed many different paintings of knights. I commented, "There must be a lot of history within these walls."

"Ali, your room is just off the main corridor and Neala, yours is farther down the hall," said our student guide. "Ali, you'll be rooming with a student from Uganda."

"Okay," I said. It suddenly occurred to me that I had never really met anyone close to my age from another country. Now, I was about to have a roommate. It was exciting. "What is her name?" I asked.

The guide didn't seem to be on the bright side. "I don't know. I was told to bring you to your room. That is all," he sighed.

Fifteen minutes later, my luggage was brought in. The handler looked at me. "You can put your things in this armoire," they instructed.

As I was unpacking, a girl came into the room.

I looked at her. "Hello," I said with a smile.

"Hello," she replied. "My name is Tibea."

"I'm called Ali."

Tibea looked at me strangely. Her voice became high as she asked, "How old are you?"

"I am four-years-old."

"I have never met anyone who is so young at this school. I'm eleven and most of the other students are near my age. Where did you come from?"

"I'm from the Albay Province in the Philippines. And you?"

"I'm from Uganda in Africa."

"How long have you been here?" I asked.

"I'm starting my second year," said Tibea.

There was a knock on the door. Tibea opened it and a large group of students entered. They studied me for a moment.

"Welcome! Who are you?" one of them said to me.

"My name is Ali and I'm from the Philippines."

A tall, slender girl was twisting the ends of her hair. "You are very young to be at this school," she observed.

"That's what I have been told," I responded.

"Oh my. We have a wee one among us," remarked a heavy set boy.

Neala taught me how to deal with bullies, so I wasn't bothered.

"And what about it? You have a problem with me being here?" I responded.

He puffed up his chest. "Just who planted you into our group?"

"My government sent me here. That is the only way you can be accepted. Are you afraid of a little girl knocking you down a couple of notches?" I asked, smirking.

"I don't think you can do anything like that. Especially being such a wee one like yourself."

"You don't mind a little competition?"

"Compete? Against you?" he scoffed. "I can do it with one hand tied behind my back!"

I knew I had pushed the right buttons. "Any takers?" I asked, looking at the group, who were watching with a deep interest.

The bully looked at me, "You're on, wee one."

A blond girl from America spoke up, "If you can count, there were only twenty-four of us enrolled in this school. Now there are twenty-five. This school is not a normal institution."

Looking at her, I said, "I'm not a normal student."

I hadn't been in this school for thirty minutes and I had already been challenged by another student.

"I like it," I whispered under my breath.

- Chapter Eleven -

Tibea sat down on my bed next to me. "Don't mind them, this is how they greet everyone," she said.

"It's okay. Even though I'm only four, they may have just met their match," I responded with confidence.

Tibea touched my hand. "I like you. You have spirit. It is going to take a lot of it to get by around here."

I smiled and turned back to the other students."Excuse me for being rude, but I don't know your name," I told the boy who had been teasing me.

"My name, wee one, is Randy Johnson," he said.

"Have you accepted my challenge?" I prompted.

"What are the terms of this challenge you are talking about?" he asked.

"If I lose, I will carry your books for a month. If you lose, you will do the same for me."

Rubbing his hands together, Randy said, "You're on."

"Now that I know what is at stake, what is the challenge?" he asked.

"Read every book in the library here. You will have one year to complete the task and the headmaster can announce the winner," I said.

Tibea looked at me with raised eyebrows. "Do you know how many books there are in the library?" she whispered.

"Nope, never set foot in it," I said.

"There are over twenty-thousand books here! The Library of Congress in the United States doesn't even have that many," Tibea said with a gasp.

I corrected her. "The Library of Congress has over thirty-seven and one-half-million books, actually."

I turned back to the group of students. "Now, Randy, are you game or are you chicken?" I knew that I was getting under Randy's skin.

"No one calls me chicken. You're on."

Shutting the door to my armoire, I said, "We will start as soon as class is over tomorrow afternoon."

Tibea looked at me. "Classes start at eight a.m. sharp. There are no bells or whistles to let you know. You're expected to be on time with no excuses. That's the way things are done here. Dinner is served at seven p.m. and there is no excuse for missing it, unless you are dying in the infirmary," she explained. The rest of the students moved out of the room so I could finish getting unpacked. Tibea moved over to her bed.

"You sure took a big bite as soon as you arrived," she said. "That challenge will be very difficult to achieve for either one of you. The whole class would have trouble trying to compete in such a challenge. Why did you make it so difficult?"

I stopped unpacking. "I like a good challenge and this one will be the most difficult at best. It may be a tie, if either one of us completes it, but now the other students know that I'm for real. If they think that I'm a pushover, they may have another thing coming."

Tibea looked surprised. "Wow, you know how to throw a one-two punch. Anyway, you should finish up. It's almost dinner time."

Tibea walked with me to the dining room. When the doors opened, I was amazed at the size of the room. Picking up several items from the food buffet, Tibea pointed at a table.

"You can sit here with me and Luwing," she said.

"Hello Luwing. My name is Ali," I said.

"I already heard," she said, turning in her chair to face the front.

"Has she got an attitude?" I wondered.

Mr. Whitaker stood up at the front of the tables. Everyone stopped talking as soon as he raised his hands. "I guess everyone has met our newest member," he began. "Miss Ali Cruz comes from the Philippines. And I'm sure you also know that she is only four s of age. She is the first and only student to ever come to our school at such a young age. With that being said, Ali, I understand that you have already challenged Mr. Johnson and he has accepted your challenge."

Mr. Whitaker paused a moment and smiled. "Now, that is what I like. A new student that hasn't been here for one hour and has already put out a challenge that will take a miracle to perform. Outstanding!"

After our meal was finished, I went to get cleaned up and ready for bed. It had been a very long day and tomorrow was sure to be just as busy.

Tibea leaned back in her chair, tapping a pen against her temple. She had a puzzled look on her face. "How do you prepare for class? Do you study before going to bed?" she asked.

"I've never been to school," I explained.

With a raised voice, she said, "Excuse me? Who taught you how to read?"

"I taught myself."

Tibea couldn't believe my answers. "Get out of town!" she shouted.

"Honest," I said, looking at her.

*****

The alarm on Tibea's clock was slamming my brain with its horrible noises. Turning over, I pulled my pillow over my head and groaned,

"What time is it?"

Tibea was getting dressed. "It's five-thirty. Get up and get dressed. Breakfast is served at seven," she said.

"Too early. The sun hasn't even come up yet," I said.

"When you're this far north, the sun doesn't rise in the winter until after eight o'clock," Tibea explained.

"Oh, I forgot." After washing my face and getting dressed, Tibea and I headed off to breakfast. As we waited our turn in the buffet line, I noticed that a big change was about to take place in my diet.

"What? No rice? It's always served for breakfast where I'm from," I said.

Tibea chuckled. "This isn't the Far East. Remember, we are in Switzerland, land of potatoes and not rice."

I looked over at everyone's plate and then back to mine. "Yuck," I said with a frown.

*****

My classes consisted of mathematics, sciences, world politics, music and art. I didn't need to take any language classes because I already knew twelve. I stepped into the doorway of my first class with pride and excitement.

"Hello," I said, projecting my voice. Everyone stopped what they were doing, looked at me, and went back to their work. It seemed that they all shared the same attitude. I sighed.

"I guess it comes from being chosen to attend this school," I said to myself. Sitting down in an empty chair, I noticed several books on a side desk, next to the wall. Not knowing who they belonged to, I pulled them over to me and started reading them at my usual pace. I had just finished the last book when the teacher, Mr. Wang, a former student from several years ago, studied me with envy.

"How can you read so fast?" he asked with curiosity.

I looked at him. "Not sure, I just can."

"Have you ever had your IQ tested?" Mr. Wang asked.

I quietly replied, "No."

"Then come with me. Class, work on the assignments that I gave you and I'll be back shortly."

Mr. Wang and I left, heading toward Mr. Whitaker's office.

"I want to have Ali's IQ tested. I was putting an assignment on the blackboard and I noticed that Ali was reading every book that I have in class. I watched in amazement as she read and understood it all. I don't have any more books on these topics that she can read." Mr. Wang explained hastily.

Mr. Whitaker set down the paper he was reading. "I see. Ali, have you ever been tested before?"

"No sir."

"Well, let's get the machine setup and we'll just check and see what kind of score you can set," he said with enthusiasm. They gave me a series of tests. I found most of them to be of little or no difficulty to me. Mr. Whitaker and Mr. Wang just looked at me with awe.

Mr. Whitaker started scratching the back of his head. "How can this be? She scored a perfect three-hundred."

Mr. Wang looked puzzled. "I did not think the machine could go that high. I have only seen it get above two-hundred and twenty-five once."

"If I could raise that number to five-hundred, she would probably take the honor."

"Ali, go ahead and go back to class. I want to have a conversation with Mr. Wang," Mr. Whitaker said. "We will talk again shortly."

Opening the office door, I turned to look at both men. "Okay," I said. As soon as I walked back into the classroom, the place became dead quiet.

With a smirk voice, Randy asked, "How did you score?"

"I scored a three-hundred," I responded.

"No one that we know of has ever scored that high," said one student. "And you're only four!" Everyone bowed down, like subjects bowing to a queen.

"You guys, stop it. You're making me blush!" I said, embarrassed. However, I was happy they were being friendly.

"Yes, your highness."

*****

"What do you want to do?" asked Mr. Wang.

Mr. Whitaker scratched his beard. "I'm not sure. Let her have all the schoolbooks to read and when she finishes those, we'll have to figure something out."

*****

I walked out of my class to head back to my room. It looked like I had just stirred up an ant pile. The instructors were in a frenzy, trying to see if I could fit in with this school.

Neala stopped by my room. "How is everything in your world?" she asked.

"Okay, I guess. I have already read all the books in my class." I said with a shrug.

"I bet that went over like a ton of bricks," Neala said, chuckling.

"It must have done something to their ego because Mr. Wang wanted me to go and get my IQ tested."

"What were the results?"

"I scored a three-hundred."

"No wonder certain people would like to get their hands on you."

She paused. "Ali, I have been called back to the Philippines on urgent business and I must leave tonight. But I cannot go unless I know for sure that you are safe. There are very few people who know where you are and I hope to keep it that way. As long as you do not leave this castle, you should not have any trouble. Here is my cell number, you can call me anytime and I'll get back to you."

"Okay. I understand," I said, feeling a bit sad.

Tibea walked into our room. "Mr. Wang asked that you return to class as soon as possible," she said to me.

Upon returning, I found several students working on different projects. Some were building things; others were working math problems.

I watched a male student from India studying a math equation on the blackboard. With his hands up to his face, I could tell that he was having problems finding the answer. I stood next to him.

"Change this to a 'y' and you'll see the answer," I told him.

He made the change and immediately, his eyes lit up. "You're correct! Why didn't I see that?"

Mr. Wang came towards me. "Ali, I have been given permission to give you every book in our school," he said, looking overwhelmed.

He opened up several closets. "There are over twelve-hundred books on these shelves. You can read them if you'd like. Please put them back in the order that you take them out."

I had a large smile on my face. I couldn't contain my excitement.

"Okay. Thank you so much!" I wanted to see what knowledge was before me. Pulling the first book off the self, I began reading with eagerness.

The room fell silent. Mr. Wang was looking at his watch. He just shook his head when I returned a book back to the shelf in five minutes and thirty-six seconds.

Mr. Wang covered his watch with his hand. "Did you already finish that book?"

"I did."

"Did you learn anything from the information it contained?" he asked.

"I enjoyed it very much. I'm a big fan of Albert Einstein. I would have loved to talk to the person who discovered E=MC^2, not to mention his theory of relativity."

Mr. Wang's mouth turned up into a smile. "Me too. He was a genius by all matters of the word." Mr. Wang sat down at his desk. "Ali, what are your goals after you leave this school?"

"I plan on returning back to the Philippines to help the people there. I have been given a gift of knowledge and it does me no good if I cannot help those who need it the most. There is so much poverty and hunger that I cannot let it go unnoticed. If I can help, then that is my goal in life."

"Good answer," said Mr. Wang. "I too, will return to my home country and do the same when I'm finished here."

All of the students started clapping. They knew that Ali Cruz would someday be a name to remember.

- Chapter Twelve -

Four weeks after I entered The World Study of Interacting Students, I read and finished every textbook the school possessed. Mr. Wang said that there was nothing that he could teach me that I didn't already know.

Several days later, Mr. Whitaker called me into his office. "I hear that you have read all the books that Mr. Wang has in his classroom. He has now released you from his class. Therefore, I'm letting you go into the school's main library and read to your heart's content. There is still the reading challenge that you and Mr. Johnson have agreed to and so far as I know, he has not turned it down. I would think that you would like to keep it going."

"I would," I replied. "That is, if Mr. Johnson still wants to take on this challenge."

Mr. Whitaker looked over the top of his glasses. "I'll talk to him and see. You may go and start your research if you like."

The librarian, a small, thin woman named Ms. Bradly saw me enter. "Please return any books after you have finished them," she said.

"I will," I said, looking at her.

Mr. Whitaker walked into the library. I heard them make several low noises. As they whispered, her voice sounded astonished. "What? She isn't old enough to."

Mr. Whitaker cut her off. "Watch and pay attention. You might learn something."

"There are so many books," I thought to myself as I headed up the stairs to the top floor. There were six floors to this library and each one was covered with books. I was so excited at the thought of so much information in one place.

I was there until almost ten at night. I suddenly realized I had completely forgotten about dinner. I read so many books that I lost count.

I knew it was time to get some rest. My eyes were trying to shut down and my stomach was growling as I walked into my room. Tibea heard the noises my stomach was making as I was setting my things down.

Sitting at her desk, Tibea put her pen down and looked up at me.

"You're up late. Where have you been?"

"I've been in the main library."

"You missed dinner," she said.

"I know, I forgot. I was studying a lot of information and forgot about the time."

"Here, I brought you something to eat. Please don't tell anyone. No food is supposed to be in our room," she said, handing me some treats wrapped in a bag.

"I won't." I savored every bite of the wonderful food she brought.

*****

The next morning, Tibea and I went to have breakfast. Carrying the bag that Tibea had brought me hidden under my sweater, I tossed it into the trash can as we walked by. Tibea saw me. "Sneaky," she said, smiling.

As soon as we entered the cafeteria's doorway, some of the students waved and whistled. Randy caught sight of me going through the chow line. He waited in his chair for the right moment to spring towards me. With a brisk walk, he stood next to where we were sitting.

"I'm officially canceling our challenge. I'm declaring you the winner, even though we haven't even started yet."

I stood up next to him to face the group. "There can be no winner. Therefore, it's a draw," I announced. Randy bowed his head and I did the same to him. Everyone started clapping.

*****

I returned to the sixth floor of the library and began where I had left off the night before. Standing in the beam of light that was protruding into the window, it felt wonderful and warm. I closed the book in my hands and sat on a windowsill staring out at the distant river. There were no clouds that I could find, just a brilliant blue color. A few birds flew by the window, floating on the winds current. I didn't hear Ms. Bradly come up the steps. She stood at the door watching me as I sat gazing out the window. She walked over and stood next to me. "Nice day, isn't it?"

"It sure is. The sunlight on the window is making it warm to the touch," I said.

Ms. Bradly looked at me. "Do you need anything?"

"No, I'm fine. I am just deep in thought. It was so quiet up here that I thought that I was alone with all these books."

I studied her for a moment. "You must get lonely here."

Turning towards me, she said, "I do. Not too many students ever come up here. They have the internet in the computer room, and most do not read from books anymore."

I looked down at my hands. "I have a soft spot for books," I said with a smile.

"I know. I have been here for forty-seven years. I spotted it as soon as you entered the library."

"That's a long time. Do you ever want to retire?"

Ms. Bradly turned away from me. "And do what? I started working here in nineteen-sixty-seven. I had just turned eighteen when I hired on. If I quit, what would I do? My whole life has been with these books."

"You have found your place in this world and you love what you do. That's all anyone can ask for."

Ms. Bradly turned her head back towards me. With a soft voice,she said, "Thank you."

I returned to what I was doing and continued pulling books down and reading them. The sunlight that was coming through the windows began turning an orange color.

"I wonder what time it is?" I headed down the steps and toward the front desk. Seeing it empty, I heard the clock chime. It was seven o'clock. That's why I was so hungry. I had skipped lunch again.

Tibea saw me coming out of the library. "I thought that you may still be there, so I came to get you. You don't need to miss dinner again."

I really appreciated her care and thoughtfulness. I thanked her and we walked to dinner together.

*****

After dinner, Tibea and I went back to our room. After a hot bath, I was relaxed and wanted to get to sleep. But that did not happen so easily. I kept tossing and turning in bed. My thoughts were running rampant. I started thinking about my mom and dad and how I sure would love to see them again. I had been so involved with my studies that I had not even thought about them for several weeks now. I wondered how they were doing. Was everything okay back home? I thought about Minda and our little secrets. It is funny how time goes by and all you can do is look back at your life in the past.

- Chapter Thirteen -

Spring was in the air and the weather was showing signs of warming up." These winter clothes will need to go soon," I said, glancing at my thick jacket. I leaned backwards in my chair, as I sat at my writing desk,

Tibea suddenly walked into our room with tears in her eyes.

"What's wrong?"

"I just received a letter from my father. I must return home to Uganda. My mother is very ill and my father has asked that I return. I will be leaving tomorrow morning."

"I'm so sorry," I said with a soft voice."When will you be back?"

"Not sure. They don't know what's wrong with my mother. I may never have the chance to return." Tibea removed her suitcases from under the bed. Setting them on top, she started to remove her clothes from the armoire. She turned around.

"I have something for you."

"It's not my birthday yet."

"I know." With a slight smile on her face, she handed me a small box.

"Well, go ahead and open it," she said. I opened it gently. It was a woven thread bracelet.

"Wow. This is beautiful. Thank you," I said.

"I made it myself."

"I will always cherish it," I said with a warm smile.

The next morning, I heard Tibea's alarm blasting its terrible noise. Turning over in my bed, I saw that she was gone. Sitting up, I stared at the chair where she had sat the night before. I pulled my knees to my chest and wrapped my arms around them. "I never got to say goodbye." A tear rolled down my face. I knew I would never see my friend again.

*****

Two weeks later, Mr. Whitaker made an announcement at breakfast. "Today is Ali's birthday. Would everyone like to sing 'Happy Birthday' to her? Ali, would you please close your eyes?" I wondered what they were up to. They all joined together and sang Mr. Whitaker said, "You can open them now,"

Before me, sat a beautiful cake with five candles on it. Looking up, I was surprised to see Neala blowing out a match.

"Neala!" I squealed and gave her a hug. "You came back."

"I said I would." I was overwhelmed. I thought I had been left all alone on the other side of the planet.

"Did you get to see my parents?"

"I did and they gave me this to give to you," she said.

I took the box that Neala held and opened it slowly. Inside was a photograph of both my parents and a photograph of Minda. I just stared at them for a long moment. The box also contained two letters. One was from my parents and the other, from Minda." Under the letters, there was a small bookmark and a note was attached.

"To Ali. From Father Bayon and Father Castillo," I read it aloud. I smiled at all the kind birthday gifts.

Neala and I went back to my room.

"Where's Tibea?" Neala asked.

"She had to go back home to Uganda."

Neala seemed a little surprised. "What for?"

"She said that her mother was sick and that she didn't know if she would ever be able to return."

Neala studied me for a moment. "I'll look into it," she said.

"Oh, please do. I really miss her."

"How's school been?"

"I don't go to school anymore."

Neala had a concerned look on her face. "How come?"

"I read every book the school uses to teach with and now I'm reading every book in the main library. I should be finished with it by the first part of summer. I think your old room is now being used by someone else," I explained.

"Let me talk to Mr. Whitaker to see if I can stay in this room with you."

Neala was granted permission to move in, since I no longer had a roommate and technically, I was no longer a student at the school, so we wouldn't be breaking any of the school rules.

*****

Neala continued to give me lessons on how to protect myself and things to look out for when I'm out and about.

"I don't like it when people get hurt," I told her.

"I know, but some people don't care what you think, and will do anything they can to hurt you or someone close to you. That's just the way this crazy world is."

*****

With the temperature warm enough to go outside, Neala discovered that the school had archery equipment in the basement. After getting permission, she was allowed to set up a target outside.

Neala stood next to me. "This is one of the oldest forms of survival," she said.

She began instructing me on how to hold, notch, and shoot a

bow. After several tries, I was able to put an arrow into the target. Not the center, mind you, but in the large outer ring. All the other students took notice of what I was doing and asked to join in. More targets were set up and Neala began teaching everyone the sport of archery.

Mr. Whitaker smiled at seeing our group enjoying the sport. He was so pleased, that he decided to have all students in the present and in the future, learn the sport. It seemed that Mr. Whitaker had some medieval knights in his ancestry somewhere along the lines and had a deep appreciation for defensive arts.

It was Pierre's turn at shooting the arrows. He notched an arrow and it flew right into the middle of the target. Everyone clapped. He notched another and did the same thing. Three more arrows and all were in the middle.

"Robin Hood!" I yelled. He bowed and everyone gave him high-fives.

After the archery lesson, Neala was called into Mr. Whitaker's office.

"Please close the door," he instructed her.

*****

Twenty minutes had passed when she reappeared at our doorstep. Leaning against the door frame, I could tell by her facial expression that something was terribly wrong.

"Ali," she said in a low voice, "I just left Mr. Whitaker's office and I had him do some digging into why your friend Tibea never returned."

"There seems to be some unrest in the community that she lives in.

A warlord has gone through her area and started a small civil war," Neala paused. "Tibea was caught in the crossfire and didn't make it. I'm so sorry to have to tell you this. I know you two had become close friends."

I yelled, "No! No, please. No!" I ran to Neala, wrapping my arms around her waist. I sobbed uncontrollably. People outside of my room heard me. It didn't take long for them to hear about what happened to Tibea. Pierre peered into my room from the hallway.

"Please tell everyone about Tibea," I said to him. It only took a couple of minutes before every student at the school was standing outside of my door. I could see that every one of them had red eyes. Tibea was one of us.

Walking into the corridor, the faculty and students had gathered around me. Turning in a slow circle, I could see the chain-link of hands joined. The bond between the members of this school was powerful. I asked for a candle ceremony in honor of Tibea. Our group disbanded.

Gathering on the main floor with their candles, the students lined up as Neala lit the wicks. Raising them into the air, everyone shouted, "To Tibea."

I raised my voice, "All she wanted was to go back home and make it a better place to live for everyone." Our band sat on the castle floor for almost an hour. We cried for the loss of our friend. The loss of her life hit me hard. I started having thoughts in the back of my mind of my own country.

A small plaque was created and hung on the wall in the main hallway, honoring Tibea.

It read, *"To those of us who want to make a difference."*

*****

Over the next several months, Neala and I had become very close friends. Even though she was old enough to be my mother, I learned a lot from her that you just cannot get from a book.

She always told me, "You have to live it in order to understand it" and I think she was right.

The summer days became longer, giving me more hours in the library to do my research. I spent most of the day there and part of the evening. Neala sat in the cafeteria every night waiting for me to arrive.

"How is it going?" she would always ask.

"It's going good. And your day?"

Neala would always reply, "Just another day."

*****

It was mid-July when I finally finished reading every book in the main library. Twenty-thousand-six-hundred and three books altogether.

Mr. Whitaker received word from Ms. Bradly that I had just polished off the last book. He sent a message back to Ms. Bradly. "I didn't think that she could do it."

A messenger was sent to my room. "You are to report to Mr. Whitakers office," she said. I thanked her for delivering the message as she scampered off.

"Ali, I have just received word from Ms. Bradly that you have read every single book. Outstanding! Would you mind if I gave you a test so I can show the powers that control this school as to why you are not studying like all the other students?"

"I do not mind at all."

"Fantastic," Mr. Whitaker replied. "I will have a set of questions from different books that are in this school. There will be several teachers and Ms. Bradly putting this test together. Give me a few days and I'll have it ready for you."

I was sitting in a very large chair at the front of the castle's entrance when Neala walked towards me. "I heard about the test that is being prepared for you. It looks like the school does not know how to handle a person like yourself," she said.

"They are preparing a test from the main library and the schoolbooks that I have read. I guess they did not believe me when I told them that I had read every book h

"If it is like the last test that I saw you take when President Datu was present, this should be a walk in the park for you."

The next morning, Neala and I were sitting in the cafeteria eating breakfast when Mr. Whitaker walked over to our table.

"Ali, the test that I had prepared is now ready for you. When do you think you would be available?"

"As soon as I am finished here."

"Come to the main library in one hour and we can put this behind us."

"Okay."

Neala wanted to see me take on the brightest school in the world.

"May I come along?"

"Oh, please do. My mother would take me to every test that I had to take. I really don't like being alone on these days."

Neala rustled my hair a little. "I understand."

A messenger was sent to all the classrooms. Everyone was to report to the library at one in the afternoon. Neala and I were making our way down the corridor, heading towards the library when I overheard another student talking.

"What's up? Why are we being sent to the library?" she asked. I overheard another girl say, "I think it has something to do with Ali."

As soon as everybody was gathered, Mr. Whitaker stood in

front of the group. "I have prepared a test made up for Ali to take. She has completed a feat that will probably never be beat again. She took it upon herself to read every book in our main library."

The students were buzzing with noise.

"I had a test made up from many different books here and there in our classrooms. Ali has agreed to take this exam. Is there anyone among you who would like to join her and take this test? There is no reward, but just knowing that you scored a credible grade is noteworthy." Several hands were raised.

"Excellent," Mr. Whitaker bolstered. A group of five of us moved to another table. "This test is slated for two hours."

We sat down and were handed a sealed packet.

"Okay everyone, you may open your packet and remove the test. Good Luck."

At fourteen minutes and thirty-six seconds, I returned the completed test from my packet and handed it to Mr. Whitaker.

"You finished it mighty early."

"I did, but not my fastest time."

Neala and I excused ourselves from the group and headed toward the cafeteria. Sitting at a table, she chuckled for a moment.

"You should have seen the look on Mr. Whitaker's face when you handed him your test. He must have thought that he had made the baddest test there ever was. Wait until he sees the results. He will probably choke or something."

In just over two-and-a-half hours, the whole school came to the cafeteria. Mr. Whitaker walked over to where Neala and I were sitting.

"Ali, if hadn't seen it with my own eyes, I would have never believed it." The five other students that also took the test walked over to where I was standing.

Joining hands, I looked at each student. "I would like to say something to the group."

Mr. Whitaker smiled. "Please do."

"To the people who took this test with me, I would personally like to congratulate you for pushing yourselves to the next level. You took on something, that you had no preparation for, and yet, you did it anyway. I hope all of you passed and even if you did not, you still challenged yourself to try to do the impossible. That, itself, is truly remarkable."

Mr. Whitaker started clapping. "Well said, Ali."

"For someone as young as yourself, you have such compassion for your fellow man. Now, as to who passed. Pierre, you scored a seventy-four. And that, sir, will be noted on your records. As to the other four, I did not expect any of you to pass, but I will make note of your endeavor to take on such a test. Since you had not studied or even heard about the material that this test covered, I would like to personally congratulate you."

"Now for Ali. She aced the test with a perfect score. No mistakes. No errors." Everyone stood and bowed.

"Oh, you guys," I said with a smile.

Mr. Whitaker began clapping. "This calls for a celebration! Tomorrow night, our whole school will have a nice meal and celebrate your accomplishment," he said.

*****

The meal that was prepared for us was fit for a king. The tables were covered with beautiful red tablecloths and adorned with all kinds of fruits, cheeses and meats. Candelabras were set every two meters apart. Standing up at the end of the first table, Mr. Whitaker began to speak again. "Would everyone please find a place to sit?"

"I am not sure if everyone here knows of the great accomplishment that Ali has just completed. What started out as a challenge for Mr. Johnson, Ali has turned into an endeavor that no one has ever accomplished before at this school. She has read every book in our vast library. No small feat by any means. So, I have prepared this wonderful feast in honor of her."

I stood up. "May I say a few words? I would like to make a toast in honor of Tibea. I had an opportunity to get to know her for a short time. I am very proud to be her friend."

The crowd all stood up and raised their cups to the sky. "To Tibea. She only wanted to make a difference."

- Chapter Fourteen -

There was a faint sound of a light knock on my door. A messenger was standing at the entrance when I opened it.

"Mr. Whitaker wants to see you in his office, right away."

"Okay. Thanks." Putting on my shoes I scampered out into the hallway.

"Ali, please come in. I am not sure how to ask someone like you this kind of question… Our school administrators are having a problem and it is with great concern about this school. And that is, what to do with you. So, I am asking you now if you would like to teach here for the remaining time that you are supposed to be here. If you accept this offer, I will have you meet the other instructors and see where they are in their studies. That way you can move about to your own liking and help other's progress."

"I would like that very much."

"When class is over for the day, I want you and all the instructors to meet here in my office so we can find out where you will fit in."

At five-thirty, all six of the instructors walked into Mr. Whitaker's office.

"I have called this meeting to inform you all, Ali will be teaching here." A murmur rose from the group.

A question was raised, "If she starts teaching here, what are we going to do? There is no subject that is taught in this school that she doesn't already know. We would basically be out of a job."

"I understand what everyone is saying," stated Mr. Whitaker. "I wanted Ali to finish out her time here."

A small, mousey man stood up. "If Ali stays, then we quit," he said. The professors began talking to themselves.

"Let's take a vote," shouted another professor.

"Excellent idea," another professor stated.

Mr. Whitaker looked at me. "Ali would you please step out into the hallway so a vote can be done?"

"Sure," I said, walking out. I headed to my room. A tear began running down my face. I felt hurt and rejected. The only school in the world for people like me and they didn't want me.

Standing at the open door to my room, I saw Neala packing her bags.

"Going somewhere?" I asked, wiping away my tears.

She looked at me. "I think our time here has run out. You have advanced farther than anyone in the world and they can't stand it. I had just left Mr. Whitaker's office when you were summoned."

Between sobs, I said, "I think you're right." I began to pack my things into my suitcases.

There was a knock on our door. Mr. Whitaker was standing at the threshold.

"Ali, I just came from my office and the vote was six to zero. I am so sorry."

Looking up at his face, I said, "It's okay. I will go back home and see what I can do to help the people from my country."

While I was packing, Neala called President Datu. She explained about the school's decision and that we needed a ride home. Hanging up her phone, she turned and looked at me.

"It will take at least twelve hours before our ride will be at the airport," she said. I tried to take a nap, but Neala could hear me crying softly. She knew that my feelings were crushed. The only school that I'd ever be able to attend was kicking me out for being too smart. Neala laid down next to me and put her arms around me. She whispered, "It's okay to cry."

Hours later I felt a tap on my shoulder. "Time to get up. The plane has arrived."

Looking at the clock, it was four-thirty in the morning. I had all my belongings in my hands as Neala opened the door. Just outside, stood everyone from the school.

I was shocked. My mouth fell open as I asked, "What's this?"

Mr. Whitaker raised his hands at the crowd surrounding him.

"Everybody here wants to say goodbye. You are about to set the world on fire, Ali Cruz, and all of us wanted to shake your hand. It has been a privilege to know you." Ms. Bradly walked forward from the back of the group and stood in front of me.

She first shook my hand, then gave me a hug. Looking down at me, she said, "In all my years, I have never met anyone like you. At first, I didn't know what to think, but as I got to know you better, I was awestruck watching you in the library. Your love for books has never been witnessed before. Until my dying days I will never forget you and everything you have accomplished here."

A tear formed in my eyes. I looked up to her and said, "Thank you."

Everyone hugged me or shook my hand. Some of the other students gave me a pat on the back. They congratulated me and wished me the best of luck.

Neala came up close to me. "We have to go. Our plane is waiting," she said.

Walking outside, I saw a beautiful old car waiting in front of the school. As we approached it, Mr. Whitaker stepped around to the driver's side. I smiled at seeing such a fine automobile. "Very nice. What year and model is this?" I asked.

He bolstered, "It's a nineteen-thirty-eight. It originally belonged to my father and after he passed away, I inherited it. I only drive it occasionally. Get in and I will take you to the airport."

After a forty-five minute ride, we rolled up to the plane. Our passports were checked in by the airport security and we were welcomed on board.

Mr. Whitaker watched us as we headed towards the gangway.

Walking over to where I stood, he kneeled in front of me and gave me a hug.

Looking me in the eye, he said, "Ali, I hope to meet you again someday. I am looking forward to seeing your name in the newspapers, television and on social media. I know that you are about to do great things."

"Thanks Mr. Whitaker. Someday our paths may cross again," I said.

"I hope so." With admiration in his eyes, he stood up, turned to walk back to his car, and I watched him as he drove away.

I grabbed my bags and boarded the plane.

"Let's go home," said Neala, smiling. The exit door shut, and we buckled ourselves in for a very long flight ahead.

- Chapter Fifteen -

After our plane landed, the pilot taxied it to a private part of Manila International Airport. Peering out a cabin window I could see a car was waiting for us as soon as we exited the aircraft. The driver, a Mr. Gonzales, was part of the president's secret police detail. Neala watched his every move, for she had seen too many of these situations where things had gone wrong. After discussing certain details that only the true secret police would know, he put her doubts to rest.

The driver stated that President Datu had two rooms at the palace waiting for us. Our luggage was taken into one of the most beautiful rooms that I had ever seen.

*****

Neala walked into her room, set her things down, and went to find the president. Seeing Mrs. Rolado sitting at her desk, she headed toward the president's office. Two guards were standing on each side of the door.

"I need to talk to the president," Neala said.

"State your name," a guard said.

"Neala."

The door was opened.

Shaking hands, Neala sat down across from the president at his desk. "Neala, I hope your flight was okay. Any problems that I need to know about?"

"Everything is okay."

"Sorry to hear about Ali. How is she taking the rejection?"

"It hurt her, but she is dealing with it."

"It still amazes me to think that she is only what five-years-old now? "He shook his head, then paused. "However, now I have new business that we must discuss. I have just been informed of another typhoon named Julio, that has developed off the southern tip of Leyte Gulf," said the president.

"It is too soon to know what the weather conditions will be like in the Albay Province."

Neala had a concerned look about her. "I will let Ali know."

"Also, give this to her. If she needs to get in touch with me. It's just like your phone," said the president, handing her a phone. Neala nodded and said goodbye.

*****

There were three knocks on my door.

"It's open!" I shouted.

"The president wants you to have a phone on your person, in case you need anything. It will make communicating with me a lot easier," Neala explained as she walked in.

"Okay, thanks," I said, taking the phone.

"Now for some bad news. We have a situation occurring off the coast in Leyte Gulf."

I sat up suddenly from my place on the sofa. My eyes widened as I looked at her. "What are you saying?"

"A typhoon named Julio is causing great damage as it heads up the eastern coast, looking for a low-pressure area," Neala explained.

"Neala, I want to go home and see my parents."

"We will, just as soon as we can," she said.

I went to find a television and get more information on the weather. The national weather station was predicting a low-pressure region would be forming over the Albay Province soon.

"That's not good," I said with worry. I curled up on a sofa

so I could watch the weather reports as they came in. I became entrenched in thought.

"What can I do to help all those people that are being affected by all these storms?" I asked, staring at the television. I shut my eyes for what seemed like a few minutes. Then, Neala tapped on my shoulder. "Are you okay?"

"Yes. I was in deep thought. What time is it anyway?" It's a little past four p.m."

Sitting up, I asked, "What? I've been asleep for almost seven hours? What is the update on the storm?"

Neala's voice was soft but firm. "The typhoon has turned and is now heading for the Albay Province. It will be passing over Bacacay in about four hours or so."

I began pacing the floors. I was having blank thoughts on how to find a solution to help. The only pictures that I could see in my mind were my family, friends and neighbors getting hurt, or worse. Neala watched me for a while, not saying a word. She had seen many people go into deep thought and not hear a word that was spoken to them. She left the room so that I could be alone.

*****

Once typhoon Julio had passed, a flight was arranged to take us back to Legaspi City.

Peering outside the aircraft windows, I could see my parents, Father Bayon and Mayor Luzon waiting on the tarmac.

As soon as the aircraft door opened, Mayor Luzon yelled up at me. "Hello Ali!"

"Hello everyone!" I shouted and raced down to greet them. I put the back side of their hands against my forehead. Seeing my parents standing a short distance from the others, I sprinted towards them. When I embraced them, I knew something was wrong.

"Mom! Dad! I have missed you terribly!" My mother hugged me tightly, but I noticed that she had been crying.

"Momma, what's wrong?" I asked.

She just gave me another hug. My father seemed very down as well. The look on both of their faces, read like a book.

Mayor Luzon spoke, "Ali, we hope you're doing well."

"I am fine," I said, growing more worried.

"We have some bad news and we wanted to tell you personally. Your friend Minda and her family suffered badly after the storm."

A look of horror crossed my face. I felt a cold chill running down my spine, just like wintertime in Switzerland.

With shaking hands, I muttered, "What do you mean?"

The mayor looked at me and explained, "Their home suffered severe damage and as a result," he paused and took a deep breath. "Minda's parents were killed by a collapsing wall."

Tears began pouring from my eyes as my whole body began to shake. With a reluctant gulp, I asked, "And Minda?"

"She is in a coma in Legaspi City Hospital."

"Please take me to her," I said, crying.

Once we made it to the hospital, the nurses on duty would not let me into the ICU. Neala and the mayor talked to the security personnel. After they explained who I was, I was granted permission to see my friend.

Standing next her, I could see that she was cut up and bruised. Tears started running down my face. "I am so sorry. I wish I could have been there."

I felt so terrible that my stomach began to ache. Bowing my head, I held her hand and began to pray. "Oh Lord, please help me with this terrible problem that keeps hurting us. I am just one child. I don't know what to do. My dearest friend in the world is laying here suffering." Everyone standing just outside of the curtain could hear me speaking softly.

I turned and looked at my parents. "Did our house have any damage?"

The mayor looked at me. "There was no damage done to your home," he said with wonder. "Your neighbors are mystified as to why every time there is a storm hitting our town, your house seems to escape any damage. They want to know how this is possible, considering the severity of the storm."

I stood next to Minda for more than an hour. I knew she could not hear me. I leaned down close to her face and whispered, "I will be back."

Looking at my parents, I asked, "May we go home?"

*****

As we drove down my street, I could see people trying to clean up their properties as best as they could. A lot of people had no home left to repair. It was just gone. Our car pulled up to my front gate. The mayor was right. Our house suffered no damage. Only those pesky leaves were gathered up in the front of the house. Inside of our home, my mother looked at me and started crying. "What's wrong momma?"

She just stood there, staring at me. Then, she kneeled down and gave me a hug. "Ali," she said.

"Momma, are you okay?" I asked. My father heard me speaking to her. "Daddy, is momma okay?"

"She is still in shock. We were supposed to meet Minda's parents at the shelter. After they did not show up, the mayor sent out a search party to check on them. That is when they were discovered. So much has happened since you left. Your mother keeps asking me where she went wrong in raising you."

"She didn't go wrong, Daddy. I have just been given a gift

that I cannot explain."

"I know. You left us at a very early age and that is all your mother thinks about," my father explained. Neala, the mayor and Father Bayon got up to leave. Neala came over towards me.

"I will be back to check on you," she promised.

"Okay."

My parents and I sat in our front room. My mother kept staring at me.

"What?"

"Minda will stay with us," Mom looked over at Neala as to give instruction. Then, she looked again at me as she pointed to Neala, "She can stay in your room, since you don't use it much anymore," she said after a long pause.

"That's fine, Momma. I would like that a lot. I hope to spend some time with her when she gets better." Tears started running down my face as I looked out our front window.

"We should not have to live this way. These typhoons are killing us and there is nothing we can do about it," I said. I went to bed thinking about Minda, her family, and all the people I knew who were suffering. I couldn't sleep. I kept tossing and turning in my bed. I began to have visions of volcanoes, black sand beaches, and the beautiful ocean waves washing up on the shore.

The next morning, Neala arrived at my door. As soon as I let her in, she spoke in a soft voice. "Good morning, Ali. What are your plans for today?"

"I want to go for a walk on a beach that has some black sand," I said.

Neala looked at me with curious eyes. "I'll arrange it, if that is what you want to do."

"It is."

Forty-five minutes later, I stood next to a grove of palm trees. I slipped off my flip-flops and took off walking. I could feel the warm soft grains of the black sand caressing my feet. Sitting down, I picked up a handful of the blackened earth, letting the dark crystals slip through my fingers. After many more handfuls, a vision in my mind began to develop. I thought that I was there for just a few minutes, but it had been far longer than that. Neala walked over to where I was sitting.

"Ali? Are you okay?" she asked. But I did not hear her voice at first. My body was sitting on the black sand, but my mind was in another world. I felt a touch on my shoulder, and as I awoke from my deep thoughts, somehow I knew what I must do.

For the next several weeks, I asked Neala when she was available, if she would she take me and my parents to see Minda. Standing next to her bed, I would hold her hand on every visit. Every couple of hours, the nurse on duty would stop to take her vital signs. I watched the nurse and asked, "Has she shown any improvement since she was brought in?"

"No, she is still the same."

I did not realize that I must have been holding her hand too tight as her knuckles were turning white. With a soft voice, I said, "Sorry."

Bowing my head, I began to say a prayer for my friend. A pretty young nurse whose name tag read "Bernadette" stood beside me. Picking up her left hand, said, "I would like to pray with you, if that is okay."

"Oh, please do." Both of us stood next to Minda for several minutes. At first, the electrical impulse in Minda's hand didn't register. A few minutes later, I felt her fingers move. Releasing my hold, I looked up at Bernadette.

"She moved her hand."

Bernadette watched for signs of brain activity. She saw it too. Minda's hand moved again. Bernadette called for more nurses.

"She is waking up. I felt her fingers move!" I said to them with excitement. They began to take her vital signs again. Suddenly, her head jerked violently.

"She must be reliving the horror of the day of the storm," one nurse said. After several more head jerks, her arms began moving erratically, then her body calmed. I watched with awe as I could see her eyes starting to open. My mother held my shoulders with a strong grip as she looked at me. I wanted to go to Minda and tell her that I had returned home.

An ICU doctor was called in. He studied her charts, then began asking Minda questions. At first, she didn't say anything.

"Can you hear me?"

Finally, she replied, "Yes."

"Do you see me?

Again, she replied "Yes."

"How many fingers do you see me holding up?"

"I see three," she said.

The doctor tested the rest of her senses and could not find any problems.

She began asking to see her parents. She rolled her head over and looked at me standing there. She kept saying, "I want to see my parents."

I couldn't tell her. My eyes teared up as I stood there looking at her. The ICU doctor left us without saying a word. About fifteen minutes later, a grief counselor was called in to talk to Minda. Standing next to her, she began speaking softly. Minda broke into tears.

"I want my momma," she said, over and over.

"They are gone," the counselor told her. I was asked to stand next to Minda. Holding her hand, she looked at me.

"Ali, where are my parents?"

The counselor's eyes looked at me and then at Minda.

"Go ahead. You can tell her," she said.

I told her the truth. She turned her head away, tuning us out. She didn't say another word. I stood next to her for almost an hour, in silence.

Neala came to my side. "We have to go," she said.

I wanted to stay with Minda, but I knew that my friend was hurting inside. I whispered to her softly, "Goodbye."

For the next several weeks I got the same treatment as before. Minda would see me coming in the door, roll over, and start shouting at me,

"Just leave me alone! I don't want to talk to you or anybody. Go away!" she screamed. I didn't say a word. I was speechless and saddened at the thought of my best friend not wanting to see me or be with me. I just didn't know what to say or do.

As I climbed back into Neala's car, she would ask, "Any change?"

"No. Everything is still the same. Neala, I don't know what to do to help my friend. Would you please take me to see Father Bayon?"

As soon as she parked, I went looking for the Father. He did not hear me enter and I watched him do his cleaning chores while humming a tune. Sitting in rear pew, I waited for him to finish. Turning, he finally noticed me watching.

"Ali, it is so good to see you," he said as I stood up in front of him putting the back of his hand against my forehead.

"How have you been?" He looked up at my eyes. "Have you seen your friend, Minda?"

"I am very troubled. She is not doing well. She told me to go away and leave her alone. My mind is so full of knowledge, but I cannot solve all the problems that I am dealt."

Father Bayon removed his glasses. "There is no human on this planet that can solve everything that is thrown at them. Sometimes they need help. That is where I come into the picture," he said.

"Father, I worry about Minda. She has become depressed. I miss her so much. I know that she has suffered a lot and I cannot change what has happened. I want to do something to help my friend."

Father Bayon looked at me. "Ali, go to her and talk to her. Tell her how you feel about her and let her know that she is not alone. She needs to be a part of something. She needs to feel wanted and not to be cast out because of her loss. It will take some time, but she will eventually come around," he said.

I looked up at his face, "I understand."

He replied, "Don't be a stranger. You know where I am, and I will help any way I can."

"Thanks again, Father."

Neala was waiting outside the church when I walked out. I saw her staring at the Mayon Volcano.

"What's up?" She pointed at the top. "Does it look different to you?"

I studied it for a moment. "It always has smoke coming from its cone. It's an active volcano," I said. Looking at Neala, I raised my eyebrows. "We don't need another disaster right now. Dealing with the aftermath of the last typhoon has created enough problems."

Neala looked at me. "Yes. You're right," she said, but I caught her returning her gaze to the Mayon. I could almost see her sixth sense is kicking in. She looked as if she knew something was not right. Getting into her SUV, she looked at me.

"Where to?"

"I would like to go back to the hospital and see Minda."

We were just a few kilometers from entering Legaspi City when suddenly there was a very loud and deep sounding rumble. Neala pulled her SUV over to the side of the road.

"What just happened?" she yelled, looking at me.

Looking out my side window, I pointed at the Mayon Volcano. "It just blew up," I said. I could see heavy black smoke billowing out of its cone. Neala returned to the road and tried to go faster, but it was no use. The heavy black smoke and ash cloud created a panic on the streets. People were scrambling. Neala drove her SUV at a very slow pace in order not to hit anyone. The streets became flooded with people trying to leave. Off to my right side I could see the police blocking the roads with x-barricades. All traffic had come to a standstill. Anyone trying to enter the city was instructed to turn around and head away from the carnage.

I told Neala, "I think that sixth sense of yours was right." She turned and gave me strange look.

*****

As we pulled up to a police officer, he instructed us to turn around. Neala pulled out her Presidential ID and after several moments, he moved the barricade and let us pass. It took us nearly an hour to get to the hospital where Minda was staying. Pulling into the parking lot, the hospital personnel were putting patients into waiting vehicles. With the ash and smoke so thick, I could barely see through the windshield. I kept staring with wide eyes at everyone trying to move about the chaos. Suddenly, I spotted Minda about to climb into a jeepney.

I jumped out of the car and ran towards her. With my shirt pulled over my mouth and nose, I began yelling, "Minda! Wait!" She saw me waving and she starts running towards me.

"Come with me," I said.

Choking and coughing, she asked, "Where to?"

"Any place but here for now. We will return as soon as we can."

"Return? For what?"

"The aftermath. Now let's go."

Neala threw her SUV into drive and laid rubber. I gave her a surprised look. She cocked her head a little and smiled.

"You go girl!" I said as I laughed.

Looking around the front passenger seat at Minda, I said, "You're going to stay with me and my parents.".

She looked at me strangely. "What are you talking about?"

" I will teach you everything you need to know in each grade level, and as we move about doing different things, you will learn more out in the field as well as in a classroom."

I could tell that she had no idea what I was talking about and neither did Neala for that matter. But they would, soon enough. We continued to drive until we reached the safety of our home.

*****

Sitting at our dining table, my mother tried to make Minda as comfortable as possible. Neala was drinking coffee when I began to explain what I wanted to do. My mother had an unusual look on her face as I started my speech. She was having a hard time trying to understand how, I, not even six-years-old, was speaking like an adult to a class.

"Neala, I will need to go back to the Mayon and retrieve a lot of samples from the lava field, as soon as it is cool enough to handle. Minda, you are going to start to work with me on a project that I am about to embark on. If you want to, I mean."

Minda gave me a surprised look. "What I can do?" she asked.

"You will help me in solving a problem that every Filipino is plagued with. Our country is devastated every time a typhoon hits us. Hundreds of people are killed by these storms and I think I know how to help stop some of this. That is where we all will need to pitch in."

Neala and my mother stared blankly back at me. I continued my speech.

"Neala, I will need to find a large lab that I can work in. We will also need to bring some specimens from the Mayon lava. The lava is made up many different compounds that come from the earth's core. One of those compounds is what I am after. I will know as soon as we can get to a lab and run some tests," I explained.

"If my theory is correct, and I know that it is, I will separate the compound from the lava and mix it with concrete. This mixture will be used to build our buildings, making them strong, and providing a better structure. We will present this idea to President Datu."

Minda just sat there, looking bewildered. "You are in direct contact with our president?" she asked with confusion.

"I am and Neala actually works for the president."

After making a phone call to President Datu, Neala came back to where we were seated. "I should have an answer shortly on a lab that you can use."

*****

In just over an hour, Neala's phone rang. Answering it quickly, she said, "Hold on for a moment."

She leaned over to me. "Ali, President Datu wants to speak with you," she said, handing me the phone.

"Yes sir."

"Ali, I have a lab set up for you in Cebu. I know that Legaspi's Airport is shut down right now, due to the Mayon volcano, so I will have a helicopter meet you on the west side of the city. Then, it will take you to the lab that you have requested. Are you sure about what all of this is for?"

"I am. The lab test will concur my findings and I can start a manufacturing facility. I will need funding to get this project started.

There will be a need to hire a lot of people to run the company as well. I will know more after the lab tests are completed."

"Okay then. Have Neala stay close to the phone and wait for my call."

Minda looked at me and then at my mother. "Mrs. Cruz, do you have any more of that coffee? I don't normally drink it, but I might have to start now after hearing all of this."

I looked at the two of them. "If there is any more, I would like some too." My mother did a double take. She poured two cups and brought them to us.

Minda sat in the dining chair with her knees pulled up to her chest, "Were you just speaking to the President of the Philippines?"

"I was. He is sending out a helicopter to pick us up and take us to Cebu. There is a lab there that I can use. Neala, do you have anyone who can go and get some of the lava samples from the Mayon?"

"Let me make some calls and check."

"Also, the president asked that you stay by your phone."

She nodded. "How much of the lava are you needing?"

"About thirty-kilograms should be enough to run the test I need."

"What time is the helicopter going to be here and where will it land?"

"It will pick us up on the west side of town. The president did not give me a time frame. I guess he will let you know when and where we should meet it."

Minda looked at me. "Am I coming with you?" she asked.

"You are."

"Momma, would you like to come with us? I know dad is still at work and won't be home."

My mother thought for a moment and nodded. "I would like that very much," she said.

Neala hung up her phone. "I have a truck and crew that will go and get the lava that you have asked for."

"Once they pick it up, have them take it over to city hall parking lot. We will meet them there," I instructed."I just hope the lava is cool enough to be handled."

*****

Several hours had passed when I received a call from Neala. "The lava is just too hot to handle right now. The scientists that are checking on it say it will take several days before we can touch it."

"Okay," I said and hung up the phone. My mother was getting my room ready for Minda. I headed outside to sweep up those pesky leaves once again. Minda sat down on the curb while I was sweeping.

Looking up at me, she asked, "Ali, what is going to happen to me?"

"What do you mean?"

"I don't want to be a burden on you or your parents."

"You are not a burden. We are best friends and we help each other however we can. Besides, I could not call myself a Christian if I just turned my back and walked away. I would never forgive myself if I did not try to help someone in need. As far as your education goes, I have your back on that. It will depend on how far you are willing to take it. Tonight, after dinner, we will start on your schoolwork. You need to learn science, math, languages, politics and history, just to name a few. We'll start with science. This subject is of high importance with the project that I am starting."

My mother had prepared a wonderful meal for us. Watching my mother's face, I could tell that she liked the idea of having Minda staying with us.

After getting the kitchen cleaned, we headed to the bedroom. I had several science books on biology, astronomy and physics stacked on a shelf. Minda opened the book I handed her.

"These look like college books."

"They are."

"But I'm only in the second grade."

"I know, but let's kick it up a couple notches."

Minda's voice grew higher, "A couple? I think you just went

into hyper drive."

"Well, let's see how well you can read, then we will go from there."

Minda began to read a biology book. I helped her pronounce and spell out the words. I repeated everything she read and explained the meanings to her. It didn't take her long to understand the world of plants.

After reading the first chapter, I gave her a short quiz on the subject matter that she had just read. She aced it.

With a large smile on her face, she asked, "What's next?"

Standing at the doors entrance, my mother listened as I explained everything to Minda. She just couldn't believe that I was teaching college level books. She was mumbling to herself, "How is this possible?" Minda and I heard her.

"Come in momma," I said. She sat on the bed with us. Listening to the lesson being taught, she put her hand on my head. Pulling me close to her, I could hear that her voice was raspy.

"Oh Lord, please take care of my child. I know you have something planned for her and may your will be done through her. She is so young. Why she was chosen is a total mystery to us. Her father and I pray your hand will be upon her always. In Jesus name." I noticed a tear in Minda's eye as well.

"He will, Momma. He will," I said, looking up at her.

Minda and I kept the studying at a steady pace. I could tell that she enjoyed the lessons. After several hours at a college level pace, Minda was getting tired and needed a rest.

"Let's set the books down for now. We can return to them later." Sitting down on the curb in front of our house, I could see those pesky leaves had gathered up again. Retrieving the broom, I headed towards the street. The wind picked up, causing the leaves to swirl around in a small circle. I thought I saw a message in them that said: "STAY." I called Minda to come and take a look at the leaves, but by the time she reached me, the wind had moved them around again.

"What is it?"

"Not quite sure, but I thought I saw a message within those leaves."

"What kind of message?"

It said. "STAY." Minda nodded her head like she knew what I was talking about. She returned to her place on the curb and I started sweeping the leaves away. I felt a cool breeze blowing on the back of my neck. Spinning around, I wanted to see what was causing the strange feeling on my skin. I saw nothing. Minda, shading her eyes from the bright sun, looked up at me.

"Now what's wrong?"

"Not sure, but I feel like someone or something is trying to tell me something."

Minda glanced at both sides of me. "That's weird."

"I know. But with everything that has happened to me over this last year or so, I am sometimes lost for words."

With a slight smile, she said, "Me too."

"Let's finish this up and go and see if my mother needs anything."

*****

My phone rang. It was Neala, "Ali."

"Yes?"

"The seismologists are saying that it will take almost a week before anyone can go and check the volcano."

"Well, there's nothing we can do about that. I guess I will have to keep on teaching my lessons to Minda." Our helicopter ride, of course, was canceled at this point.

"Keep me posted."

My mother overheard my conversation. "Who's that?" she asked.

"It was Neala. She is on the Mayon with a group of scientists. She just stated that it will be at least a week before we can gather up some of the lava that I need." My mother stood there scratching her head and mumbled something about lava.

*****

Minda and I kept up on her studies. Working for most of the days on different subjects, I could see that she was coming along very well.

"Minda, would you like to take a high school exam and see just where you are compared to the other students?" I asked.

She smiled. "I would."

"Tomorrow is Friday. The three of us can go over to the high school and take a test." My mother liked the idea. She was excited to see how my teaching of Minda was taking shape.

*****

Friday morning, we jumped out of bed and got ready for a very interesting day. The smell coming from the kitchen was wonderful. My mother had prepared breakfast for us, consisting of rice, sweet sausage,eggs and coffee.

"Momma, are you coming with us to the school?"

"Yes I am. I want to see how Minda is doing in her studies."

Minda had a large smile on her face. She liked the thought that my mother and I had taken an interest in her.

We finished cleaning up the kitchen and headed towards the high school. Entering the main building, we made our way to the principal's office. The secretary sitting at the front desk asked, "May

I help you?"

"My name is Ali Cruz. This is my mother, and this is Minda Torres. I would like to have the principle give Minda a test that is usually given to the graduating students."

"A test? Why would we do that? Just how old are you two?"

"I am five-years-old and Minda is six."

"Young lady, I think that you are in the wrong school. You two are too young to be here."

I happened to notice a plaque on the wall by the front counter. It states, *"Through these doors walk the smartest people in the world."*"I see a plaque on your wall over there that states *"the smartest students go to this school."* Care to challenge that statement?" The Principal, Mr. Sanchez, was sitting in his office when he overheard my challenge. Standing against his office door, he looked at me for the longest moment.

"I remember you from last year. You will have to excuse my secretary. She is new and doesn't know about you."

"I understand. I have a friend here with me that would like to take a high school test that you would give to the graduating students." The secretary looked puzzled.

"Mrs. Diaz, this is Ali Cruz. She is one of the smartest people in the world." Mrs. Diaz mumbled something under her breath.

"When does your friend want to take the test?" asked Mr. Sanchez.

I gave him a smile. "Her name is Minda Torres, and she would like to take it right now if that would be possible."

"Minda, I have heard Ali speak for you, but I need to know if it is what you want and not Ali."

Minda paused for just a few seconds. Looking up, she smiled. "I would like to take your test. It is something I must do for myself."

Mr. Sanchez liked Minda's answer. "Okay then. Let's do it."

*****

"Now Minda, you will have exactly one hour and thirty minutes to take our test. Are you ready?"

"I am.

"Okay then. You can go into that room over there, so you can be alone."

Heading towards the door, she looked over at me. I gave her a thumbs up and a smile.

*****

At approximately one hour and two minutes, she exited the private room.

Walking over to Mr. Sanchez's desk, she said, "Here it is."

We waited for almost twenty minutes before the door to Mr. Sanchez's office opened. He walked over to where we were seated.

"Minda, I have some great news. You passed it. I only found two wrong answers. Not bad, considering that there were over one hundred questions on this test."

"Ali, did you have something to do with Minda's education?"

"Well, I had a hand in her lessons," I said.

Mr. Sanchez just smiled. "I thought so."

Minda had a very large smile on her face. "I just passed the biggest test that I have ever taken!" she said with glee.

- Chapter Sixteen -

Neala had gotten word from the scientists that I was cleared to venture close to the volcano. Sitting at the dining table folding laundry, my mother overheard my conversation with Neala.

"You go and get what you need. I will be here waiting for you," she said.

"Okay momma. We won't be long."

Looking out our front window, I saw Neala pulling up to the front of my house. She beeped her horn and I kissed my mother on the cheek.

*****

Jumping into Neala's SUV, I buckled myself into the passenger seat.

"Hey Neala. How are things?"

She looked at me. "Everything is good."

Neala started her car. Pulling away from the house, I put on my happy face.

"What's first on our agenda?"

"We are going to meet one of the scientists that has been working on the Mayon at City Hall in Bacacay."

After we had arrived and all introductions had been made, he was delighted to meet with me. He kept saying, "I have wanted to meet you ever since I heard about your great gift." He started asking me questions about why I was gathering up the lava. I explained my intent for the project.

"If everything works out, I will need many kilos of lava. I will know soon, once I can get the lava to a lab for analysis."

He just stared at me. "I too have lost my family due to a typhoon," he paused, "I would like to work with you on your project."

"Please give me your phone number so I can get in touch with you," I said. He wrote down his phone number. "How is this going to work with your current job?" I added.

"Like I said, I lost my family to a typhoon three years ago and I am not currently married. I only contracted to do this job for the government. After the contract is up, I am free to apply for another job."

*****

We all headed towards the south side of the Mayon. After arriving on site, we were met by a military detachment. The MP asked for identification. Neala showed her ID and we were allowed to pass through with no more problems.

With a point of my finger, I showed everyone the lava that I was interested in, which was about halfway up the volcano. Finding a path on the side of the volcano seemed to be another problem that we had to tackle. Parking at the bottom of the Mayon, we met a group of scientists under a small tent. We were each given a pair of special shoes, as well as gloves to wear. Lava has very sharp edges and can cut like a razor blade. We had to take precautions. Picking up some small pieces of the lava, I noticed that it was still very warm to the touch. All samples were placed into a special container provided by the scientist so that it would not set fire to anything it came in contact with.

Returning to Neala's SUV, I said, "Let's go and pick up my mother, then we can head over to the lab in Cebu."

*****

Everyone stayed with Neala as I went inside my house to retrieve my mother. Before leaving, momma glanced at herself in the mirror by the front door, and all I heard was, "hum." She glanced in the rear of Neala's SUV. "So, this is the stuff that is going to save the Philippines?"

I looked towards her as she got into the front seat with Neala. "Yes."

*****

As soon as we arrived at Legaspi City Airport, the lava container was removed and loaded into the cargo hold of a jet as we boarded the plane. Minda could not believe that she was on an official government aircraft. I watched as she went from window to window, looking at everything on the outside excitedly.

Sitting next to me, my mother took my left hand and began squeezing it hard.

"It's okay momma," I reassured her. She noticed my knuckles were turning white.

"Oh sorry," she said and then she let go. Looking into her eyes, I held her hand and smiled.

"I wish your father was here with us."

"Me too."

My mother looked out the side window. "I would like to take a vacation, just the four of us to someplace different one day," she said.

"I like that idea Momma. Let's plan on taking a trip."

Looking at me, she said, "I am not sure how we could afford such a trip though."

"I don't think we will have to worry about finances in our future." My mother gave me a puzzled look.

Our flight time to Cebu was less than one hour. As soon as we landed, the plane was taxied to a remote part of the tarmac. Neala said, "We have to wait for the airport security." While Neala dealt with the police, we were led to a waiting car. A truck was brought in and my lava samples were unloaded. Once everything was secure, our convoy headed towards Caplin Mining Co.

The attendant at the front desk called Mr. Caplin, letting him know that our group had arrived. Mr. Caplin introduced himself to us.

He studied the four of us. I could tell that he didn't know what to think. He looked at Neala. "I have everything set up for you."

Neala gave him a smile. "I am not the person that you need to speak to." Neala introduced me. He gave me a peculiar look. With a polite smile, he thought about his next question. "I have to know. Just how old are you?"

"I'm five."

"I wasn't told that a young person like yourself would need my lab."

"I get that a lot. Don't worry, I know what I am doing." Scratching his head, he walked away.

*****

Donning a lab coat and goggles, I began mixing compounds together. I noticed my mother had fallen asleep on a sofa that sat in a small room off from the lab. Neala was in security mode, making sure that we would be safe. As soon as she felt comfortable with our surroundings, she left to take care of some business and would be back later. Minda put on a lab coat, goggles and hearing muffs. Standing in front of a full-length mirror, she turned around several times looking at herself.

"I look like a mad scientist out of a science fiction movie for little people!" she said.

Glancing in her direction, I said, "You do!" We both started giggling like the little girls we were. "Do you want to cook somebody or tie them to a rack and raise them up to a lightning storm?" I joked. She did a zombie-like walk with her lab coat dragging the ground behind her. We began giggling again and laughter filled the room. I knew in the back of my mind that I was only five, but I also knew that our Lord gave me a purpose to help the people of the Philippines any way I can. I truly enjoyed those rare moments when I got to be a five-year-old.

"Minda, please put the lava samples into this machine. It will crush the rock into a powder," I said. Examining the mixture under a microscope, I showed it to Minda and explained what I was after. I then explained what it was to be used for.

Minda showed excitement in her voice, "Do you think it will work?"

Looking at her, I said, "Yes, I believe so." By mixing the compound from the crushed lava with a base of cement, I worked the mixture together.

"Let's give it a try."

Minda carried a bucket that contained seawater to the table. Adding seawater to the mixture, I was able to make the special compound and join a group of concrete blocks together. I asked several technicians from the next room if they would help me build two walls onto a cart so I could maneuver it. Next, we had to build a wall using my special compound. A second wall was built using ordinary cement. Both walls had rebar inserted, just like any normal construction would.

"Now this will have to sit for at least twenty-four hours so the concrete can harden," I said. Minda took off her mad scientist outfit, putting it back where she got it.

"What now?" she asked.

"We need to find a place to stay."

*****

Knocking on Mr. Caplin's office door, I was summoned inside. "Mr. Caplin, do you know of some place that we could stay the night?"

"Yes. I do. It is not too far from here."

Waking my mother, we gathered up our things. Mr. Caplin taxied us to a hotel that was close by.

With a special account set up for me by the government to use to purchase things that I may need, I secured two rooms by having the desk clerk at the hotel scan my cellphone screen. The accommodations were nice, and the restaurant was supposed to be excellent.

My phone rang. On the screen was Neala.

"Where are you?" she asked.

After receiving directions, she put the information into her phone. As soon as she checked in, the four of us ate until we thought we were going to bust.

Neala looked at the three of us sitting at the table. "I am going to bed," she said with a yawn.

I replied, "Tomorrow should be very promising." We all went off to bed to prepare for the next day.

*****

Arriving at Caplin Mining, I saw Mr. Caplin walking towards his office. "Mr. Caplin, do you have any way of hitting these two block walls that I had built with a horrendous wind? Something like that of a typhoon?"

"I sure do. I actually have a wind machine that can produce a wind force up to four-hundred kilometers. No man-made structure has ever withstood such a force," he said.

"Can we put my mixture to the test?" I asked. He nodded.

Cameras were set up surrounding the test area to film the extraordinary event. A hooking brace was attached to hold the base blocks, since they were just sitting on the floor. My wall was on the left and the regular wall, on the right. Mr. Caplin threw the switch to the wind machine. At wind speeds of the fiercest typhoon ever recorded in the Philippines, my blocks didn't move. The speed was increased. The wind machine topped out at two-hundred-and-fifty-eight miles an hour, or four-hundred-and-fifteen kilometers. Standing behind a secured wall with observation windows, I could see that my wall was not moving, but the other wall had started to disintegrate, scattering concrete material all over the room. Parts of the wind tunnel structure were starting to show signs of fatigue. As soon as the wind machine could be shut down, we examined the concrete blocks. My wall looked as though nothing had happened to it. The ordinary concrete wall had collapsed into pieces. Deadly projectiles were hitting the rear wall, leaving deep dents. Mr. Caplin was amazed at what he was looking at.

"You made the compound to glue the blocks together?" he questioned.

"Yes."

"I would like to know more about your ideas."

I sat in his office for nearly an hour, discussing the plans for my invention. Walking out, everyone heard him say, "Ali, Caplin Mining is here if you need us. I know we can do business together."

"Thanks, Mr. Caplin, for letting me use your lab and equipment. When I do get my business started, we can talk again," I said.

*****

Everybody was curious about what we had discussed. "I will tell you once we board our plane," I announced.

As soon as we were airborne, my mother excitedly burst out, "Now tell us!"

"He wanted to know if his company could be part of the plans that I have."

My mother raised an eyebrow at me. "And what great plans do you have?"

"Well, this trip and the testing that we just completed were the results that I was looking for." All eyes were watching me.

"I am going to start a company in Bacacay to make the compound that I used to glue the concrete blocks together. We are going to need a building to start our company in. Then, we will need security, workers, and trucks to make our business grow." I saw everyone scratching their heads. "Now just hear me out," I said.

"Okay, we're listening," they said with their eyes fixed on me.

"I am wanting to sell our product to all building contractors in the country. The profits that we generate will be used to help people in need. If we can build a better home here in the Philippines that can withstand the typhoon winds, just think of how many lives we can save."

Neala liked the idea that I had in mind. "Ali, that sounds all well and good, but how are we going to pay for starting up this company? You are talking about a lot of money."

- Chapter Seventeen -

Neala's phone rang. "Yes sir. I can be there in about two hours."

She hung up and called me. "Ali, I have to go to Manila for a few days, and I won't be back until the end of the week."

"Okay," I said curiously.

*****

Boarding a government jet, Neala headed to the Presidential Palace. Walking into the president's office, he said, "Shut the door, please."

"How can I help?"

"I need to take care of this mole that is in my administration," he told her with a serious expression.

"I see. I thought that problem was already taken care of."

"I thought so too. But I just learned that my private conversations are being leaked out to the press and to just about anyone who wants to know my business."

"Have you checked your office for bugs?"

"That is why I asked you here. Can you take care of my problem?"

"I can, sir." Leaving the office, Neala headed towards the Secret Service Headquarters.

It did not take her very long before she had the necessary equipment to detect any bugs and plant a few of her own.

Scanning the president's office, she found three. Carefully removing them, she placed them in a lead-lined container.

Ever since Ali had come into her life, Neala had a suspicion of who the mole was. Doing a little detective work of her own, she planted her own bugs that could record video. It didn't take long for her plan to work.

The president and Neala watched the video of his personal secretary making a call on her cell phone. "They found the bugs," she said into her phone. Hanging up, she placed her phone back into her purse. By putting a trace on her phone, Neala sent a group of police officers to the address of the person (or persons) on the other end of the line.

After a half hour had gone by, Neala received a phone call.

"We have the person in custody. It was none other than the secretary's son. He has a computer full of all kinds of information and maps; notes on Ali."

Neala spoke into her phone, "Good work."

Neala left the president's office, heading straight toward his secretary's desk.

Standing on the side of the desk, Neala barked out, "Stand up."

Turning in her chair, the secretary asked, "What for?"

"Stand up," Neala demanded. "Or I will drag you out."

"How dare you!" she wailed. Neala was on her like a cat on a mouse.

Bending her over her desk, she pulled the secretary's arms behind her back, placing a set of handcuffs on her wrists.

"What is the meaning of this?" she demanded.

"I found your bugs and planted my own. Your son has been arrested as well."

President Datu made a call. A team of agents walked into the outer office. Neala motioned to them.

"Take her away and question her. We need to find out everything there is to know about who she is working for and what plans they have."

After returning to the president's office, he sat in his big chair and put his feet up on his desk. "Nice work, Neala. You handled that job quickly."

"Thank you, sir. We will still need the information about who is behind this and why they are looking at Ali."

For the next three days, Neala kept up the interrogation of the secretary and her son. She discovered the answers that she needed to bring closure to the situation. After a careful examination of her son's computer, they had all the information about who was behind spying on the president.

*****

Neala led the group of trained military personnel to Salazar's Palace. After completing a successful raid, Neala returned to President Datu's Office.

"I found the brother of Salazar trying to take over his business. It turns out that your secretary is a first cousin to someone in your opposing party. Now all the pieces in this puzzle fit."

President Datu took a moment to take in all the information. He nodded and thanked Neala.

"Neala, how is Ali doing?"

"She is fine. Her test at the lab was conclusive. The compound she has invented will save a lot of lives from the typhoons."

The president was amazed. "How does it work?"

"It will be mixed with cement and used to put walls together, It is so strong that the wind machine that Caplin Mining has, it did not phase the wall that she had built. The ordinary wall standing next to hers collapsed into thousands of projectiles. I was awestruck, witnessing her wall withstand a wind more powerful than the strongest typhoon."

"Excellent," President Datu stated. "What is Ali's plan with her mixture?"

"She wants to start a company making the stuff and shipping

it out to every province in the country," Neala explained.

The president stood in front of his office window. "I can see the importance of this new product. If buildings don't collapse, a lot of lives can be saved."

Neala responded to the president, "The next hurdle that Ali has to overcome is financing her company. To get started, it is going to take a lot of money."

President Datu went to his desk and handed Neala a flyer that he had just received from his mail room. "I don't normally get mail like this. As soon as I saw it, I thought of Ali."

The flyer was titled, *"The Battle of the Minds"* and it read:

> *This contest will consist of a preliminary test, as well as an advanced test. All applicants will take their first test at the local university or college in their area. Then, they will be brought to Manila to take a test at the University of the Philippines. Each country that will be participating in this event will send their top scholars to Tokyo for the finals. They will challenge each other until one person is left standing. The top prize is ten-million U.S. dollars. The contest will start on September first, two-thousand and fifteen. You can pick up an entry form from any school. The cost to enter this contest is four-hundred and fifty pesos."*

President Datu looked over at Neala. "What do you think?"

"I can almost guarantee that Ali won't turn down such an event. This will be a challenge to her, and she loves to be challenged."

- Chapter Eighteen -

The time I took to work with Minda and her studies, my mother enjoyed the idea of us girls being at home. One Wednesday evening, I heard a knock on the front door. Opening it, I saw Neala with a teasing look on her face. I studied her for several seconds.

"Why are you smiling like that?"

"Ali, I think I may have found a way to raise the money that you need to start your company.

I became excited. "How?"

Everybody gathered around Neala. Opening her notebook, she pulled out a flyer that came from the president's office. She began to read aloud about a contest, a worldwide academic challenge in which the prize was ten-million dollars. My eyes widened as I listened.

With shaking hands, I grasped the flyer from Neala. All I could say was, "How do I enter?"

"To officially start, you will have to go to your nearby college or university and take a starter's test. Then, the people who passed will move on to the next level."

My mother could not believe what she was hearing. My hands were still shaking as I handed her the flyer. As she read it aloud, Minda was smiling.

Neala headed to the kitchen to retrieve a bottle of water from the refrigerator. I could hear her talking to herself. "When it comes to a battle of the minds, I saw Ali smoke the best of the best already," she muttered. Hearing her words warmed my heart.

The next question that my mother wanted to know was, "Will you take on this challenge?"

I quickly placed my hands under my armpits to try to keep them from shaking. I said, "Oh yes. I am not going to back down from a ten-million-dollar challenge. If I win, the money will start our company, put a lot of Filipinos to work, and help our country to battle the typhoons."

With a smile from ear to ear, I looked into my mother's eyes. "I got this."

My mother continued going over the information, "The finals will be held in Manila, at the University of the Philippines. Then the field is narrowed down to just the top three. They and their families will be flown to Tokyo to take the test of all tests."

"Now, stop teasing me. I want to do this."

Neala walked back into the living room. "This has not gone out to the public as of this afternoon. You will soon hear about it on television, newspapers and the radio. Giving out the exams and everything to do with it will cost four-hundred and fifty pesos. The first leg of this contest will start on September first. You have to sign up by August fifteenth. You have three weeks before you can even sign in," she explained. "In the meantime, Ali, I have been scouting around the area looking for a building that you could buy. I have found three that look promising."

Suddenly, we heard the front door opening. Turning, I saw my father entering.

Running to him, I shouted, "Daddy!" I gave him a big hug and a kiss on his cheek.

"Hello Ali," he said as my mother gave him a hug and a kiss. Seeing Minda, he said, "Hey Minda," as he gave her a hug as well. She smiled. It gave her comfort knowing that she was still part of a family.

Studying his surroundings, he asked, "Am I missing something?"

"We are just discussing a building that I am planning to buy," I exclaimed. The look on my father's face was classic. "You don't say."

My mother replied, "Ali is wanting to start up a company and needs a building to make her product that will save the Philippines."

My father shut the door and sat his things down. "You most definitely have my interest. Now I want to hear all about this idea of yours."

Everybody gathered around the sofa. I began to explain what I wanted to do. "The money from the contest would be more than enough to get the business started."

"Daddy, would you consider being the president of my company?"

"Well, you will have to win that contest before I would even consider quitting my job."

"I understand."

"Neala, when can we go look at the buildings that you have spotted?

We need to see if they are in decent shape or if they would have to be torn down and rebuilt."

"We can leave now if you would like."

"Dad, are you up to looking at a few buildings with us?"

"Give me a few minutes to get cleaned up," he said.

*****

The first two buildings were in horrible condition and would have to be torn down and rebuilt from scratch. Neala removed the listings from her shirt pocket.

"The third structure is on the south side of town, about three kilometers away. It was called Bondoc Concrete. It fell on hard times and had to shut down."

A concrete company building sounded promising. "May we see it?" I asked with an optimistic tone.

Pulling up to the outside gate, I could see that it was locked. Standing next to the fence, I knew immediately that it would do just fine for our needs. "I wonder how much it is selling for," I said.

Neala looked at her paper again. "They are asking four-million pesos," she said.

"I like it. I would like to see the inside."

Neala pulled out her phone and called the number on the for-sale sign.

Hanging up, she said, "The owner says that he can be here in one hour."

"We can wait."

*****

At a little past three, a black SUV pulled up next to Neala's car. A big man with long gray hair hanging over the collar of his black suit stepped out. Standing next to his car, he asked, "Who is interested in my property?" All fingers pointed at me. The man's left eyebrow raised up considerably. "Okay, I can take a funny joke, but you guys are really trying to pull my chain, right?"

Neala stepped up to the man in the suit. "No joke. I can assure you, she is interested in your property." Turning, he looked straight at me. "Just how old are you?"

"I am five-years-old, and I would like to see the inside of your building. I am going to start a business and I need property to build on."

The big man was hesitant about pulling keys from his pocket. I watched his lips as he mumbled something and shook his head. Opening the gate, he said, "Let's go to the front of the building and I will let you check it out."

"Okay, thanks," I said. Returning to our cars, we entered the property.

The five of us progressed to the front of the building. I tried to envision what this building would look like with my new company headquartered here while we waited for the big man to unlock the door.

"This is the main office area and through those doors over there is the warehouse area."

My father and I entered the rear of the building. I could see the potential of this building. I looked at my father. "Daddy, what do you think?" He looked at me.

"Well, what are your plans for your business?"

I explained what I wanted to do.

"I see. Then this property would work for what you want."

I looked over at the man who was selling the property. "What are you asking for this property? Are the taxes paid up?" He looked at me strangely.

"Are you sure that you are just five-years-old? You talk and act like an adult."

"I am sure." I could hear everyone in my group giggling.

My mother put her hands on my shoulder. "Ali, you are going to get that question a lot and you had better get used to it."

The businessman scratched his head. "Did I just miss something?"

Minda stepped in. "This is Ali Cruz."

The man raised his eyebrows at me. "Well, I'll be. I heard about you. Father Bayon has talked about you to our congregation. He tells us that you are going to bring great things to our country." The wrinkled forehead told me that he was suspicious of my motives.

"Forgive me for being a little nervous. When everyone pointed their fingers at such a young person and said you wanted to buy my property, my first impression was that you guys were going to try to scam me. The price was four-million pesos, but since you are interested in it… and if you do what they say you are going to do, I will let you have it for three million pesos. This place used to belong to my brother and his wife, but he was killed last year during Typhoon Henrietta. I bought the place from his widow."

Minda spoke up, "I lost my parents to the last typhoon. I hope Ali can help in building better houses. Strong enough to keep them from falling on top of us."

"Ali, my name is Dr. Med Montoya. I am the chief surgeon at Memorial Hospital in Bacacay. Buying real-estate is a hobby of mine and I think I would like to make a proposition with you. If you can design a stronger, better home for the Filipinos, I will donate this property to you for your new business. All I ask, is that you mention in your advertisements that the property came from me. I am a businessman you know."

"I think we can come up with a business slogan that would benefit your business, "I said happily, grateful for his generous offer

Dr. Montoya put his hands into his pockets. "When are you planning to start up your business?"

"I have a major contest that I must enter in the first week of September. Money that I may earn, would be enough to get my business started."

"That must be some contest."

Minda jumped into the conversation. "It pays ten-million U.S. dollars!" she said.

"Oh my, that would most definitely start a company. You could hire a lot of workers and buy trucks."

I looked up into the eyes of the doctor. "Now you sound like me. I mentioned the exact same thing to President Datu," I said.

Dr. Montoya looked surprised. "You know the President of the Philippines?"

"I do. And I have him on speed dial."

Dr. Montoya let out a surprised chuckle.

"Well folks, I do not want to keep you any longer. Ali, you can call me anytime and we can get together and fill out the papers. Here is my business card and here is my hospital number," he said. Shaking his hand, I thanked him for meeting with us.

*****

Heading down the highway towards our home, everything finally sank in. "We just got a building for free," I said, realizing how blessed we were. "The money we saved can be used for other expenses." But then I began to have second thoughts about what had just happened. I looked over the seat at my parents and Minda. "I feel like I just took advantage of someone and I don't like this feeling in my stomach."

My mother tapped my arm. "I know exactly what you are talking about. It is never a good thing to take advantage of someone. No matter who it is," she said.

"If I win this contest, I will pay him for his building. I cannot and will not use anyone or anybody to move forward on this."

My father looked at me and smiled. "You are going to be a very smart business woman."

- Chapter Nineteen -

The Battle of the Minds contest began to hit the evening news channels. All the radio stations began broadcasting the information over the airwaves. Minda and I were studying when we heard the television spokesperson begin talking about a contest that had never been done before. The co-anchor responded, "I wonder if Ali Cruz knows about this contest."

The anchor woman stated, "If she doesn't, it won't be long before she signs up." That caught my mother's attention. My mother came rushing to our bedroom.

"Ali, have you heard the news?"

"I just did. It's now official. I have two weeks before I can sign up."

My mother stared at me. "How does a television station in Manila know who you are?"

I raised my shoulders. "I don't know. It may be because of when the president came down to visit me."

Minda gave me a high-five. "You rock girl!" she said, and we giggled excitedly.

*****

For the next several days, everything was quiet at home. That's when my world suddenly became a media frenzy. News reporters had opened our front gate and were knocking on our door. My mother was standing next to me when tons of microphones were shoved into my face.

"Ali, are you going to sign up for the Battle of the Minds contest?"

"What are you going to do with the money if you win?" I waited until I could find a break in all the questions that were volleyed at me.

"If I could ever win such a contest, the prize money would be put to good use here in my province, helping the people here at home."

"And how are you going to do that?" was the next question thrown at me.

"I will state what my plans are, if and when, I win this contest. You must not forget that this contest is worldwide. There are a lot of very smart people on this planet. I will have more to say after the contest," I said.

My father had enough of all the questions. "Thank you for asking," he told the reporters.

My mother looked at me. "You handled yourself very well," she said. Walking away, I could hear her mumbling, "I am not surprised at anything you do anymore."

*****

The next morning, my parents, Minda, and I headed to the local college. A banner was on display just inside the doors. It was large and very colorful. It read:

> *"The Battle of the Minds Contest. Watch the finals on your local television. This event is open to anyone and everyone. The cost to participate is only four-hundred and fifty pesos."*

The sign said to go to the library to sign up. I saw an adult woman walking towards me in the hall.

"Excuse me, where is the library?" I asked her.

Pausing, she leaned over a little. "Are you planning on taking the test to enter the Battle of the Minds Contest?" she asked smugly.

"I am," I said. Another teacher noticed the attitude that the woman displayed.

Walking up next to us, he said, "Wipe that smile off your face. That young lady has an IQ so high that the test instruments cannot read it."

"Who is she? Ali Cruz?" the woman chuckled.

"As a matter of fact, that is exactly who she is."

The smile disappeared immediately. "The library is over there, just down the hall," the woman said.

Looking up at the man, I said, "Thank you."

As soon as I entered the library, I could hear people whispering, "That's Ali Cruz." Someone asked, "Who is Ali Cruz?"

A teenager responded to the question, "One of the smartest people in the world. Her IQ is off the charts." Everyone watched with amazement as I paid my entry fee to the clerk and turned in my application. A group of students clapped as I walked out of the building. Minda and I did a high-five as the four of us headed home. Later that night, I sat watching the television with my parents when my name made the headlines.

"Its official," the news reporter began. "Ali Cruz has turned in her application for the Battle of the Minds Contest. The first leg of this competition is at the local college or university. It will consist of two-hundred questions. This test will cover every subject from elementary grades to college level and it will have a time limit of just two hours. A score of ninety or higher must be achieved in order to advance to the next level. All contestants must take this test on October first of this year. Good luck to all!"

I went to tell Minda. She looked up from her book. "I heard," she said, clutching her book up to her chest. "I wish I could take the test."

I knew where she was coming from. "You can. There is nothing stopping you," I said with a smile.

"Yes. There is. Me. I did okay on the high school test, but this is college level and I don't know any of the information they will cover."

I gave her my school teacher smile. "Not true. What books do you think I have been working with you on? All of them are college level!" Minda closed the book that she held in her hands.

"Do you think that I could ever take such a test?"

"I do. I really do think that you can pass it," I said.

Minda smiled. "Thanks for believing in me."

"You're welcome. If you want to take this exam, we can go tomorrow, and you can sign up."

She looked at me. "I don't have any money to pay for it," she realized.

"I do. And I've got your back."

The next day, my father had to run some errands around town. That left my mother, Minda, and myself to go to the university without him. My mother asked me softly, "Is she ready for such a test?"

"It's kind of hard to say, but I cannot not blame her for wanting to try. This will boost her morale."

My mother patted my head. "Oh Ali, this is why I love you so much. You are always thinking of others."

The three of us walked into the school's library. Leading Minda to the front desk, I said, "Tell the clerk what you want." The clerk looked over the counter to see us two small girls standing there.

"May I help you?"

Minda looked up at the lady. "I would like to sign up for the Battle of the Minds Contest."

"The entry fee is four-hundred and fifty-pesos."

Minda smiled. "I know. Here is my money. Where do I fill out the application?" she said. We moved out of line to a small table against a wall. After filling it out, she handed her application to the clerk. It was officially stamped.

"Be here in two weeks on October first, at eight-thirty in the morning," said the clerk.

"We'll be here," Minda replied, smiling.

Minda went into full-time student mode. Every day, she was pacing back and forth, back and forth, with one book and then two, in her hands.

"You are going to be fine," I told her.

"I know. It's just that I need to study a lot."

"Now you look like me when I took on the book challenge in Switzerland." Looking over the top of her book, she smiled and went back to reading the chapters. "I will leave you alone to your work, if you need help, just yell."

My mother saw me walking out of my bedroom. "How is Minda?"

"She's fine. Right now, she's elbow deep in her studies and I didn't want to bother her. She is taking this contest seriously."

My mother smiled. "Aren't you?"

"I am, but Minda is trying very hard. I hope that she doesn't get disappointed if she does not make it to the next round."

My mother patted my head and said, "She'll do fine. She wants to be like you so much. I see it in her every time you two are together."

I looked up at her. "I have noticed it as well."

My mother prepared a very nice meal for us. After the kitchen was cleaned up, Minda went back to our room to hit the books again.

Looking at the wall clock, mom said, "It is getting close to nine p.m. Go and tell Minda to get ready for bed. I don't want her burned out before she even starts."

"I will Momma." Walking into our room, I saw Minda lying on her bed with a book opened, covering her chest. She had fallen asleep studying. "Done that before," I said, talking to myself.

This pace kept up for the next two weeks. The last night before our big day at the university, Minda stayed busy cramming more information into her brain.

My mother walked into our room. "Okay girls, I don't get to be a mother figure very often with you two, but tonight, I am. You cannot think clearly if you don't have enough sleep. Therefore, I'm laying down the mother's law. Close the books, get ready for bed, and we will leave in the morning together."

After she walked out, Minda and I agreed. We giggled at the 'mother stuff' she had said. Minda smiled. "She is right. I like her being my mother, a lot."

I smiled too. "Yah, she's not bad at all."

"Good night."

*****

The next morning, the alarm was going off at six a.m. With eagerness, we were both dressed and got ready for breakfast. Minda sniffed the air. "A cup of coffee would sure be good right about now," she said.

"I believe you're right," I said. Walking into the kitchen, we saw mother had been preparing breakfast..

"Coffee is made," she said. "I am starting to learn the habits of you two."

With the kitchen cleaned and teeth brushed, the three of us headed off to take on the world, or at least, it seemed that way.

*****

The contestants were asked to go to the auditorium and wait until our names were called. Looking around, I didn't recognize anyone there. Suddenly, I saw a man dressed in black attire, walking right past us. It was Father Bayon.

With a raised voice, I said, "Father, we're over here!"

Turning, he saw me waving at him. Moving his way past a couple of students, he sat next to me. I took the back of his right hand and put it to my forehead.

"Good morning, Father."

"Good morning Ali, Minda, and Christina."

Minda leaned over in her chair. "Father, I am taking this test as well," she announced.

"Good for you. I've always said that a mind is a terrible thing to waste."

The dean walked up to the podium. "Good morning. If you are not here to take the test and you are not the parents of a student who is taking the test, please exit the room."

After a few minutes of getting everything in order, the dean spoke into the microphone. "There are seventy-nine people who have signed up, so please raise your hand when your name is called. We must have an accurate count of people."

After roll call, he instructed, "Everyone go to the cafeteria. There are alphabet letters assigned to each table. Find the letter that goes with your last name and take a seat. This test will start momentarily."

Everyone scrambled to the cafeteria to find their table. My mother and Father Bayon moved back as a herd of people wondered about. Finding our seats, I spoke to a girl who was sitting next to me. "Are you ready for this?"

With a shaky voice, she said, "I guess so."

The dean stepped up to the microphone. "Okay everyone. In front of you is your test. Do not open it until I say so. Do not talk to anyone, or you will be asked to leave. Do not look at anyone else's test. We have monitors walking around to keep a watch on you. You have two hours to complete this test. If you are finished, raise your hand to let the monitor know that you have completed the exam. Get up from your seat and walk out of the room. Do not talk to anyone.

If you do, your test will be discarded. Do you understand?"

Everyone in the crowd confirmed that they understood. "Okay then. Open your folders and begin. Good luck," said the dean.

At fifty-eight minutes into the exam, I raised my hand. A monitor came over to where I was seated. I handed her my test. Standing up, I left the room without saying a word to anyone. I didn't want to lose by doing something foolish. I headed towards the exit with my mother and Father Bayon in tow. I think I had a smile from ear to ear as we headed towards the main doors of the school.

My mother showed eagerness on her face. "How was it?" she asked.

I looked up at her. "It was easy. Minda may stumble a little, but I think she might just ace this one."

Father Bayon lowered his head to look into my eyes. "Did you have anything to do with her teaching?" he asked.

"Maybe," I said, with a giggle.

Smiling at me, he said, "I thought so. Our Lord is showing you a light. May your path be lit and prosperous."

"Thank you, Father."

Just after the two hour mark had passed, we headed back into the school to find Minda. She had just turned the corner of the hall when she spotted us. Hustling over to where we were standing, she exclaimed, "I just finished the hardest test ever!"

"You sure did at that."

My mother looked at Minda and me. "When will you know if you passed it or not?" she asked.

"They said to check late this afternoon or come back tomorrow," I responded.

Minda became very excited. "I don't think that I can wait until tomorrow."

"I don't think I can either. Let's go and get some lunch and then we can discuss our next plan."

Father Bayon liked the idea. "We can go and get a pizza at Angelica's place. Her mango shakes and pizzas are to die for," he said.

After a wonderful lunch, we thanked Angelica, and said our goodbyes to Father Bayon. Devouring the last of my mango shake, I watched as he flagged down a padyak (a bicycle with a cart attached) so he could make his rounds at the orphanage and hospital. Climbing into the cart, he yelled at us, "Let me know what the test results are. I may have to use something like this in a future sermon."

"I will Father, just as soon as we find out."

*****

Upon returning home, I noticed those pesky leaves had gathered up for another sweeping. Minda sat down on the curb, watching me.

"How do you think we did?"

"Not sure."

"Did you see the look on the faces of those college students that we walked past? It was priceless!"

"I'll say. They looked like they were going to pass out or some thing. Us elementary school kids, here we are taking a test that they wouldn't touch in their whole life."

A little after four, my mother came to where we were playing.

"I like to see you two being just normal girls. It makes my heart warm," she said. We didn't say anything to her. We knew exactly what she was talking about.

My mother seemed more excited about checking our test scores than we did. "Do you girls want to go and see the results of your test?" she asked.

Minda became eager with excitement. "I would love to," she answered.

I just looked at them both. "Nah, I think that I will just stay home." Minda looked shocked and sad. I waited a moment and then laughed. "Hey, I was just messing with you!"

She gave me one of those mischievous smiles. "Thought you had me going for a moment, didn't you? Fooled ya!" I messed with her hair and she did the same to mine as we headed out the door.

Walking into the front of the main school building, a note was pinned on the school bulletin board. It read:

*"Go to the auditorium for the
Battle of the Minds Contest results."*

The three of us headed towards the back of the room.

The dean walked up to the podium. Speaking into the microphone, he said, "Please, quiet down everyone. If I call your name, come up and get your packet. It will have everything in it for the finals to be held in Manila." My name was called. After returning to my seat, I watched Minda's reaction. I wished her name would be called. That would be something that she would never forget. They were getting down to the last names on the list.

"Minda Torres, please come up and get your packet," the dean said.

She jumped up. "I got one!" she wailed with excitement. Pushing past me, Minda's face was beaming with joy.

"I got a packet, Ali," she said with disbelief.

"Go and get it!" I told her. She ran up the stairs to the stage, thanking the dean.

"Okay folks, that concludes this portion of the program. If you received a packet, arrangements for travel to Manila in October are inside."

As we got up to leave, I noticed a group of the older students, staring at us. I overheard a college-age girl say, "I know about Ali Cruz, but who is the other girl with her? And who is teaching her?"

A male student standing next to her said, "I can almost bet you that Ali had something to do with her lessons." A third girl among the group looked at Minda as we headed out of the school.

"I want some of that; wherever she is getting her lessons from!" The four of us did a high-five and left.

- Chapter Twenty -

With just two and a half weeks before we needed to be in Manila, Minda asked me if we could go and use the university's library. "We will have to go there and see if we can get permission to use it." I had a sudden realization and began pacing the floor.

Minda watched me with concern. "What's the matter?"

"We don't have a way to get to Manila," I said, pulling out my phone.

I hit the speed dial and tried to call Neala, but all I got was, "This mailbox is full. Try again later." Hanging up, I hit another button. After several rings, President Datu answered.

"Hello Ali. How was your first contest?"

"Everything went well. I am supposed to be in Manila on the twentieth, but I cannot get in touch with Neala."

"She is out of the country at the moment, and not expected to return until the eighteenth."

"I see. How am I going to get to Manila?"

There was a pause on the line. Then, President Datu said, "I will have a plane there on the nineteenth. I will let you know more about it as we get closer to the date. If I hear from Neala, I will pass your message along."

He began speaking again, "Also, while I have you on the line, you know that answer that you gave me about Leyte Gulf and the treasure there?"

"I remember."

"Well, you are correct in your answer. I had it checked out and the treasure was exactly where you said it would be. I still haven't figured out how you knew. We'll keep in touch," he said pleasantly.

My mother heard me talking on the phone. "Who is that,

dear?" she asked.

"It was President Datu."

"You called the President of the Philippines?"

"I did."

"And what did he have to say?"

"I told him that I needed a plane to take us to Manila on the twentieth."

"What? You just called the president and ordered up a jet to take you to Manila?"

"Yep, pretty much."

Minda overheard me speaking. "Now that is totally awesome!"

"Momma, Minda and I would like to go over to the university and see if we can use their library."

My mother was mixing food together with her hands as she asked, "When are you wanting to go?"

"As soon as you are available to go with us," I said.

She nodded. "Give me a few minutes. I am preparing our dinner for tonight."

*****

Minda waited for our mother to finish up. She then hurried outside to flag down a trike, (a motorcycle with a cart attached to its side).

"Take us to Zamora Memorial College, please," she said.

The three of us were off on another mission. I walked up to the counter where we had signed in to take the test. The same lady looked at us as we stood there.

"May I help you?" she asked.

"We would like to use the school's library," I said.

"Are you a student here?"

"No."

"Then, I'm afraid that is not possible. You must belong to the university in order to use any of its facilities. It's a school policy that must be strictly adhered to."

"We will just have to go to the public library," I said. Minda was puffing up over the rejection from the university.

"All I wanted to do was look at their books," she sighed.

I knew where she was coming from. "I know, but all schools have rules that must be followed," I said.

The local library, while okay for most people, was lacking in information that Minda was going to need to pass the next exam.

"Minda, I think that you are going to have to continue with the books we have at home. I just don't see anything here that will help you."

"I think you're right," she agreed.

"So far, what I have brought home has gotten you this far. If you need more, we can go over to the cybercafé. You can use their computers to surf the net."

Shrugging her shoulders, she looked at her hands. "I know that we are in a modern era, but I just like the feeling of a book in my hands." I looked at her hands, then at her face.

"You think like I do," I said, smiling.

*****

Word was sent to all the contest winners that had received a packet. The contestant's trip to Manila would be covered by the province where they lived. Minda read the letter that we had received.

"Looks like a bus trip is in order for the contest winners. Are we actually going on a bus?" she asked.

"Not that I am aware of. If we do, we will definitely have to leave on the eighteenth instead of the nineteenth."

*****

The morning of the eighteenth came, and I had not heard a word from Neala or anyone in the government. Minda walked into the kitchen to where I was making coffee.

"Morning. So, what's on the agenda for today?" she asked.

"Well, I was hoping to hear something from Neala, but my phone has not rung once. I hate this waiting game to find out if we have transportation or not."

My mother walked into the kitchen where we were seated. "Coffee is made," I told her.

She looked at both of us sitting at the table. "Thanks. Isn't a plane supposed to pick us up on the nineteenth?" she asked.

"It is."

"Well, your father will be here this afternoon. He took off from work a little early. His boss didn't like it too much, but it's not every day that your daughter goes to Manila to take on a nation."

I looked at Minda. "We can go over the cybercafé and use their computers. Someday, we'll have one of our own." I said. My mother got up to pour herself another cup of coffee. I heard her mumbling about cybercafés and computers.

*****

Sitting at the cybercafé, my phone rang. It was Neala. "The plane will be at the airport at nine a.m. tomorrow, I will be pick you up at eight. Have your bags packed," she said.

"I will."

Minda looked at me. "Who was that?"

"Neala. It's a go. A plane will be waiting for us." She couldn't have smiled any wider. I saw white teeth from ear to ear.

A little after two p.m., my backside was tired of sitting.

"Let's go home," I told Minda. I thanked the clerk and paid for our internet usage.

Minda stood out the door of the café. Looking at me, she said, "Let's walk. It's not that far and it would be good for a change." Several padyak drivers offered us a ride but we declined and walked home.

Entering the front door, I noticed my father was home. "Daddy, you're home!"

"Hello Ali," he said, giving me a hug. Seeing Minda standing next to me, he said, "Hello Minda," and gave her a hug as well. Looking back at me, he asked, "How's everything in your world?"

"It's fine. We have a ride to Manila for tomorrow. Neala will be here at eight in the morning and our plane leaves at nine."

"Your mother told me that you called up the president and ordered a plane to take us to Manila."

"I did."

My father walked off towards his bedroom, chuckling and mumbling like my mother does. "My five-year-old daughter calls the President of the Philippines and orders up a jet to take us to Manila."

I looked at Minda. We did a high-five and giggled.

"I'm hungry. Let's make lunch," I said.

*****

I was up before seven. Walking into the kitchen, I could see Minda was already preparing breakfast and the coffee smelled wonderful.

"What's up girl?" I asked.

"I am going to see a big city that I have never been to before and compete against the top students from our country, in the Battle of the Minds Contest," she mused. "Win or lose, I still win."

"I know, that's right. Win or lose, we still have each other." My parents walked into the kitchen, seeing smiles on our faces. They both seemed puzzled. "What's up?" My mother asked. As she saw that the table was set and breakfast was already made, she added, "A big thanks to whoever cooked breakfast!"

"Minda did."

"Not bad. Not bad at all," mother said.

Heading outside, I noticed those pesky leaves had gathered up again in front of my mother's store. Picking up a broom, I hit them with a vengeance. Looking up from my task, a dark shadow from Neala's SUV was coming towards me. Moving to the curb, she stopped in front of our house yelling through the passenger's window, "Are your bags packed?"

"They are. I will get the others." I ran inside to get my family.

*****

On our way to the airport, Neala told me about her trip to Moscow.

"I hope it was successful."

Smiling, she said, "It was. We are in a bit of a hurry this morning. The plane has to leave Manila as soon as we land. After the contest, we'll catch another one to come home."

I looked at Neala, "Thanks for everything."

She smiled. "I feel like your step-mother or aunt. I like the feeling a lot," she said. She patted my hand.

I thought to myself, "It sure is nice to have both my parents, Neala and Minda with me. Life doesn't get any better than this."

*****

Once we arrived in Manila, a private car was waiting for us. Reservations were made for us at a beautiful hotel, not far from the university. A separate bedroom, off to one side of my parent's room, was for Minda and I. There was excitement in Minda's voice as she called dibs on the bed closest to the window.

"I want to lay here and see the city lit up at night."

"Yes, Princess Minda. Will you need your bath water drawn as well?" I chuckled.

"Not right now," she answered. We both giggled and headed into my parents' room. Sitting at the table that sat next to a large picture window, I heard a knock on the door. My father climbed off the bed to answer it. Neala was standing there with a thrilled look on her face.

"We have reservations at a dinner comedy show tonight. The acts are outstanding, I hear. It should be a lot of fun."

I noticed that Minda was enjoying herself. "I'm game," she said.

"I have never heard of such a place, but hey, I'd like to try something new."

My mother looked at Minda and me. "As long as these two are not up all night, then we're in," she said.

Neala looked at us. "We should be back by nine," she said.

*****

The dinner and the show were fantastic. Minda and I kept making faces like the comedians did while telling their jokes. We laughed at each other. I noticed my parents were watching us and I saw them smiling. I even caught Neala with a smile on her face as we headed back to our hotel.

Standing in front of our rooms, Neala walked by us. "Be ready by eight a.m. We have to find a place to park and the building where the contest will be held," she said.

Lying in my bed, I watched Minda stare out the window. She was mesmerized by all the colorful lights that lit up the sky.

"We need to get some sleep. Tomorrow will be here soon," I told her. She slowly shut the drapes.

Lying there in the dark, I tried to focus my eyes on the ceiling.

I heard Minda say, "Thanks Ali. Thanks for everything. You're the best friend in the whole wide world." Listening to her words, I felt a little tear in my eye and that made me feel wonderful.

"You're welcome," I said, smiling.

Chapter Twenty-One

Minda had her eyes glued on the size of the University of the Philippines. "I have never seen a school this large before."

"The castle that I stayed in Switzerland did not cover this much ground. It must take half an hour just to get across campus," I said.

After parking, we went to find the main office. After asking several students, we were pointed in several different directions.

"I guess the young college students of today don't know the four points on a compass," I joked.

An older man walking at a quick pace moved around us.

"Sir, excuse me. Can you tell me how I may find the office for the Battle of the Minds Contest?"

"I sure can. I am heading there myself. Just follow me." We followed the man right to the building where the battle was about to start. I saw the sign that read: *"Sign in here."*

Pointing a finger, I said, "There!" Minda and I scampered off to the registration table. Standing in line, I leaned over to see just how long it was going to take to register. "Minda, would you hold my spot? I have to go use the restroom." I raced to the bathroom and headed back. Hurrying to the line, I could see where Minda had moved up quite a bit. Another line had started and many of the people that were behind us, moved to it.

We had just walked up to the table when several announcements were made over the auditorium speakers.

Minda looked at me. "What did they say?"

"Something about registration."

The student behind the table yelled, "Next!"

"Name?"

"Minda Torres."

"Got it. Here are your papers, please hand them to the monitor assigned to you when you are finished."

"Next. Name?" the student yelled.

"Ali Cruz."

"Hey, Miss Cruz! We have been expecting you. Here are your papers and when you are finished, please hand them to your monitor."

There were hundreds of people, ranging in all ages. "This is going to take a lot of time," I whispered. Returning to where my parents and Neala were standing, I opened up my packet. A note attached to the documents read that I was in group C. It also stated to proceed to the cafeteria and find our groups. Minda saw that she was in group T. A map inside the packet pointed the way to the cafeteria.

Studying the map, she said, "We have to go this way." Making our way through the hallways was difficult. Minda and I were small in height compared to the majority of people taking the test. Neala took over and politely moved a few bodies out of the way so we would not be trampled. We separated as we searched for the alphabetical letters on the tables.

Minda and I did a high-five. Both of us said, "Good luck."

An announcement came over the PA system. "All parents and relatives, please leave the room. We need contestants only."

A petite woman with long black hair that nearly touched the ground picked up a microphone. "Welcome to the Battle of the Minds Contest," she began. "This test will take approximately three hours to complete. When you are finished, return your test to its packet, then hand it to your monitor and leave the room. There will be no talking while you are in this building. This exam starts in five minutes. Good luck to everyone."

"You may open the packet that is in front of you." I looked at my test with a fierce determination. I furiously read and wrote down answers. In approximately one-hour and thirty-two minutes,

I raised my hand and gave my test to my monitor. I left to find my parents. Standing outside the rear of the building, they stared at me.

My mother gave me an ear full. "Well, how did it go? Was it hard? How did you do?" she asked.

"It was suppose to be a three-hour test. I didn't have any problems with it." I reassured her.

*****

At the three hour mark, the petite woman picked up the microphone.

"Pencils down. Please place your test inside the packet, then hand your test to your monitor and leave the building."

Minda was shaking when she walked out. "I don't think I passed. Some the questions I did not know the answers to."

"I know. Some were tricky on how they were worded."

I heard Minda's stomach making growling noises. "Can we go and get something to eat? I'm starving," she said.

"I like that idea. Where to?"

Neala pointed down the street. "I know of a place that makes excellent pizzas. And it's not far from here."

My mother smiled. "Lead the way."

*****

After eating a wonderful lunch, we headed back to the school. A sign posted in the cafeteria stated to go to the auditorium. Finding seats for five, we waited anxiously for the announcements.

The petite woman picked up the microphone. "Everyone, please be seated and quiet down. I want to thank everyone for taking this exam. There are only three places that will move on to Tokyo. If I call your name, please stand so everyone can see who you are." The first two names were announced. Neither one was mine nor Minda's. We looked at each other. We held hands as the speaker announced, "Will Ali Cruz please stand?" I stood up slowly.

"Everyone, this young lady not only passed this exam, but she did it in just one-hour and thirty-two minutes! It was checked and rechecked. She didn't miss a single answer. We have never seen anything like this before. Ali, just how old are you?"

"I am five-years-old."

A murmur came over the room. No one knew how to handle the fact that a tiny young girl had done so perfectly on such a difficult test.

"Will those who have been called come forward? We need to get some information to send to Tokyo." Minda was smiling at me, but I knew that deep in her heart she was sad. She didn't make it. After giving her a hug, I headed to the table of the judges.

"We need to see your passport. If you don't have one, you cannot leave the country."

"One moment please," I said. "Neala, do I have a passport?" She pulled one out of her bag and handed it to me. I passed it to a security officer. She scanned it and handed it back.

"I see that you have done some traveling. How was Switzerland?"

"I liked it a lot. I didn't get to see much of the country. The castle that I stayed in was very remote," I responded.

"We will see you in four weeks in Tokyo. The instructions, location where you will be staying, and information about transportation to and from the contest are enclosed in the packet that I just gave you. How many are coming with you?"

"There will be four, plus me."

"Okay then. We will have the travel arrangements made. They too will need a passport to leave the country."

"Thank you."

Turning around, I headed straight to Neala. "We are going to need passports for my parents and Minda."

"How much time do I have?"

"Three weeks."

Neala's eyes widened. "That will be tricky, but I think I can handle it."

*****

On our trip back to Legaspi Airport, everybody was quiet. I noticed that Minda wasn't looking out the window. I moved in the seat next to her.

She began to play with her hair. "What's going to happen to me now?" she asked.

"What do you mean? We keep moving forward. This journey we are on is not over by a long shot. We still have to make the money to start a business. You still need to work on your studies. We have a building to start with, but it is going to need a lot of attention."

"What happens if you don't win in Tokyo?"

"Not sure, but I guess it can happen. Never thought about it much. But I would probably feel like you do right now. Hey, let's not talk about something that has not happened yet. Let's stay positive. Okay?"

Staring down the walkway inside the plane, a seed of doubt had been planted. I think I needed that pep talk more than she did. The thought of losing it all at the last minute never occurred to me. That 'what if' was now moving around inside my head. "I have to stay focused on the positives, not the negatives," I kept telling myself. I never told anyone about what I was thinking. I had never been so scared in my life. Now the thought of losing everything was playing in my head.

*****

Landing in Legaspi City, Neala retrieved her SUV. Everyone was silent. I think it was the quietest trip I had ever been on. Minda headed straight to her bed once we arrived home. I could hear her crying. I figured she needed some alone time. Shutting the door, I walked over to the sofa and fell asleep.

*****

I could smell fresh coffee being brewed. I saw my mother in the kitchen preparing breakfast.

"Hello sleepy head," she said. She didn't ask why I was sleeping on the sofa; she had also heard Minda crying. She understood how Minda felt.

I walked over to my mother and gave her a big hug.

"I love you Momma."

Minda walked into the kitchen. "Are there any more hugs left? I could sure use one about now," she said. All three of us hugged each other tightly.

My mother looked at both of us. "No matter what happens in the future, I want you girls to know that I'm here and will be here for you anytime."

- Chapter Twenty-Two -

After winning the local contest and making the trip to Manila to take the country's top spot in the Battle of the Minds Contest, the final leg of the competition was nearly at hand.

There was a heavy knock on the front door. I opened it to find Neala, standing there with an armful of items. Scanning our living room walls, she found one she liked and began removing pictures. She started to hang a white sheet. My mother walked in. "What's up?" she asked, watching Neala.

"Passport photos. Is everyone here?"

My mother responded, "Yes."

"Okay then. Don't smile or make the peace sign or anything like that. They will reject your paperwork. You will also need to sign this document."

After Neala had left, Minda's eyes were nearly shut. "That flash was bright," she said.

It took Neala seven days on the passport acquisition, but she came through on getting the documents needed for my parents and Minda to travel to Tokyo with me. As I handed Minda hers, she smiled brightly.

"How do you look on your passport?" I asked Minda.

"It looks like a mugshot from one of those American gangster movies I read about," she said, laughing.

"I know. Mine does too."

My father looked at his photo. "I look like that gangster you were just talking about. You know, rat, tat, tat." He acted like he was holding a machine gun in his hands.

Neala saw an opportunity. "Be careful. I just busted someone who looks like you," she joked. My father closed the passport quickly.

Neala laughed and pointed her finger like a gun.

"Gotcha!" she said, and everyone got a laugh at my father's facial expression.

Neala pointed out, "We will be in Tokyo for three days and we'll be staying at a very nice hotel, close to the convention center where the contest will be held. Our flight from Manila will be approximately seven hours. Bring reading material if you have any thing. Our day is going to be a long one."

The airtime to Manila seemed short compared to what was ahead. Minda had gotten over being upset about her loss in Manila. She had finally accepted that she had a lot of learning ahead of her. After winning in the locals, she knew that she just may be a contender on a national level someday. And that I didn't doubt her. She was very intelligent.

We boarded Japan Airlines. Once we were in the air, the flight attendant came around asking if we wanted something to drink. Minda spoke in Japanese, asking if she had any orange juice. The attendant spoke back to her in Japanese. I watched in fascination as Minda carried herself like an adult.

Smiling at her, I said, "Very good. I didn't know that you could speak Japanese!"

"When I found out that we may be going to Japan, I started learning a few phrases."

"So far it seems to work."

Landing at Haneda Airport, I ran into none other than Randy Johnson. The young man that wanted to take on the reading challenge with me at the School of Interacting Students.

"Hello Ali."

"Hi Randy."

"I guess you made it to the top in the Philippines," he said.

"I did. And you?"

"The same. Where are you staying?" he asked.

"The Royal Park Hotel."

"Cool. I'm with my parents and we had to find a room farther out in the city."

After we had caught up on the gossip of things, Neala gestured for me to come on.

"Well, I'll see ya!" I told Randy as the five of us were hustling off to the baggage claim.

Our hotel was very nice, with a modern look. Arriving on the the fifteenth floor, Minda and I discovered that we had adjoining rooms, with my parents on one side and Neala on the other. Once we entered our room, Minda looked at the bed location. "Flip you for it," she said, pulling a coin out of her pocket. "I want the window view," she said as she tossed the coin into the air.

I yelled, "Tails!"

Her coin hit the floor and spun around a couple of times. "Heads! I win!" she said smiling.

I flopped onto the other bed. The door between the rooms were left open.

"What's for dinner?" I yelled. Neala walked through her doorway into our room. "What's your poison tonight?"

"I am not sure. Let's ask Mom and Dad."

The three of us scampered over to the next room. My mother spoke up. "Pangasius, from the Mekong Delta."

Minda responded, "Wrong country."

I glanced over at her. "Very good."

Neala came up with an idea. "Since we are in Japan, let's eat at a Japanese restaurant."Everyone agreed that was an excellent idea.

Neala pulled out her cell phone, and in minutes we had reservations at a Japanese Steak and Sushi Bar. Sitting on a small pillow with our legs crossed, Minda and I practiced up on our Japanese language skills as we ordered our dinner. I heard Neala order something in Japanese as well.

Looking at her, I said, "I didn't know that you could speak Japanese."

Neala tilted her head towards me. "I have many talents."

"You do at that!"

After a wonderful meal, I thanked Neala for suggesting it. The five of us wandered back to our hotel to get some sleep. Tomorrow was going to be a very long day.

*****

At seven thirty in the morning, the five of us were standing outside the hotel. Neala put fingers to her mouth, making a loud whistle. She waived her arms wildly as she hailed a cab. The driver gave us a strange look as our gang climbed into his very small car. Packed like sardines, Neala gave the cab driver our destination and we headed to the convention center. Arriving a little after eight, I could see that the sign-in line was through the main entrance doors and people were standing outside the building.

I thought to myself. "This contest starts at ten and I'm not even inside the building."

As soon as I stepped into the doorway, I saw Randy Johnson talking to an older man. It was Mr. Whitaker.

Walking up to him, I tapped on his arm. "Hello."

As he spun around to see who was touching him, recognition set in.

"Ali! I was hoping that you would be here." My entourage stood next to the table with me.

"Mr. Whitaker, these are my parents and my best friend, Minda. You already know Neala. Everyone, this is Mr. Whitaker. He is the headmaster of the school that I attended in Switzerland."

"Mr. and Mrs. Cruz, while Ali only attended our school for a very short time, she pushed the bar to a whole new level. What

I mean is, her gift of knowledge is far superior to anything that I have ever seen. Ali, I hope you do well," he said.

"Thank you," I said and moved toward the registration table.

The way the finals were held was completely different than the previous contest. All of us were allowed to sit in front of the stage. At ten a.m., Mr. Whitaker took to the stage and made the announcements.

"Once the rules have been read, we will begin to call names. When you hear your name, please come forward to the stage. You will be asked a series of questions, covering many different subjects. You may also have to work out mathematical formulas or work on science problems. Good luck." The participants took to the stage. Some didn't make it through the first round.

A blackboard was brought onto the stage with a mathematical equation on it and the contestants had five minutes to figure out the answer.

That kind of problem solving eliminated many of the participants. My name was called. Walking on to the stage, I could hear murmurs coming from the crowd. I didn't know that I was known throughout the world.

I answered the questions and solved the science problems. After the first day of competition, half of the nine hundred and twelve participants were eliminated.

*****

Day two arrived and the questions became a lot harder. I watched as more of the contestants were eliminated from the field.

"Ali Cruz, please come to the stage," said the announcer. I answered the questions just like before and I threw in a little extra flair by making jokes. I got a chuckle from some of the senior professors in the audience.

The judge warned me not to do that in the future. I saw Minda smiling. At least she enjoyed it.

*****

Day three was the finals. As the day progressed, the field of thirty-two was narrowed down to just two: a boy from Russia and me.

A different speaker was brought in to ask the final questions. A coin toss was performed to see who would go first. I chose heads and won.

As I listened to the speaker's voice, I was having a difficult time trying to understand her because of her accent. She asked a series of questions and I answered her without any mistakes. However, on the last question, I didn't hear the question correctly because of the noise coming from a hot air balloon that was flying overhead, I gave the wrong answer. I realized that I had just made the most serious mistake in my life. It cost me the contest. Neala caught on to what happened, and she rushed towards the stage. I stood there staring at nothing. Covering my face, tears started to flood my eyes. My world crumbled right there on stage, in front of the whole world. I lost the only contest that I needed to win to move my goals forward.

The Russian boy saw what happened to me and corrected himself to give the right answer. Suddenly, the whole place came alive with confetti and streamers. Loud music began playing. After that, he was announced as the winner of the Battle of the Minds.

Neala walked me off the stage to my parents.

My mother put her arms around me. "Let's go home," she said.

Everybody knew what this meant to me. I let them down. My dreams of helping the people of my homeland were shattered.

Minda knew where I was coming from. She too had the same experience just weeks before.

*****

I was lying in my bed, facing the wall, when Minda walked in.

Sitting on the edge of my bed, she said, "Hey girlfriend." Turning over to look at her, my eyes were red and my pillow was soaked with tears.

"Everything will be okay. We still have each other."

"I know. It's just that I wanted to win so badly. Everybody was counting on me. Now, I have no money to start with."

"This little talk reminds me of just a few weeks ago. You came to me with the same answers I'm giving you."

"I know. But I would like to be left alone right now," I said. Minda understood and left.

The next day, I saw my mother in the kitchen preparing our meal.

"Where is daddy?" I asked.

"He left to go back to work."

I knew that she was disappointed by my loss, just by the sound of her voice and the way she kept her head down while cutting up a head of bakchoy for a sinigang soup.

My mother looked up at me. "The news reporters keep knocking on our door. They want to talk to you for a news story."

"I hope they go away. I don't want to talk to anybody right now."

"You can stay hidden for a while, but eventually you are going to have to face the world," she said.

"I know, but not right now."

Looking out the front window, I could see Minda sweeping up the leaves that had gathered up in front of our house. Turning away, I went back to my room and shut the door.

*****

For the next several weeks, I didn't leave the house. One day, there was a loud knock on our door. My mother had her hands clinched tightly. She did not like it when the reporters were so persistent. My mother opened the door. Putting all my effort into voice recognition, I could hear Neala's voice. Standing in the doorway of my bedroom, she studied me. In a demanding voice, she said, "Ali, let's go."

"Go where?"

"To see Father Bayon."

My mother patted my back as we headed out the door.

My mother whispered to Neala, "Thank You."

The two of us entered the front door of St. Rose of Lima Parish Church. There was Father Bayon busy cleaning the pews. Hearing the door open, he turned and saw me. "Ali."

"Hello Father."

"How are you?" he said.

"I'm okay, I guess."

He noticed the sound of my voice. "Come here and sit with me. Tell me what is happening in your world."

"I failed, Father."

"Failed?" He asked with a surprised voice. "Failed at what?"

"I didn't win the contest. The money was to be used to help the people."

"You haven't failed my child. Not by any means. You are only human. You have suffered a setback, but that is all. Now you must pick yourself up and push forward again."

"But I don't have a way to make the amount of money that is needed."

"There are always ways to accomplish your goals. Keep your faith child. Say your prayers and everything will work out."

"Thank you, Father, for listening to me."

"My pleasure. Ali, my door is always open. Anytime you need to talk to someone, I am here for you."

"Thanks again, Father."

- Chapter Twenty-Three -

For the next several months, my life as a young businesswoman was on standstill. With no money, the building that was donated to me sat abandoned. My mother would sometimes catch me staring out the front window. She would stop and ask what was on my mind.

I would tell her, "It's my dreams. You know, the ones where the people would not have to suffer from these storms." She would hold me tightly.

"My Ali. How on earth you became so intelligent at such an early age is beyond me."

"I know, Momma. I sometimes wish I didn't have this brain. Just being a normal child would be fine, I guess. But this is not my case. Father Bayon says that I just had a setback."

My mother looked down at me. "I think he was right," she said. "Your world was moving like a high-speed train and now you're stopped on the tracks." She kissed the top of my head and left. All of my previous thoughts about how to make the money needed to push forward is now a blank space in my mind.

Minda and I took over the cooking duties for the evening meal so my mother could have some time to herself. She was watching the television when the screen began showing a weather alert.

"A super typhoon, that has been named Carlos, has formed off our coastline," the reporter said. Alarmed, I turned around.

"Minda, can you finish cooking this so I can listen to the weather report?" I asked.

"Sure."

Standing next to my mother, I put my hands on her shoulders.

She looked up at me. "It's happening again," she said. I just squeezed her shoulders gently. She could tell what was about to happen by the look of the horror on my face. And yet, I couldn't do a thing to help. We watched anxiously with our eyes glued to the television screen. The weather woman shuffled her notes.

"It's too soon to tell where this storm will make landfall. Start making preparations now, so you can make it to safety." Minda stood next to me and I could see a tear in her eye.

"Not again," she kept saying. "Not again."

Our evening meal was hard to swallow after hearing the bad news. I kept stirring my food around on my plate.

My mother noticed what I was doing. "You need to eat. You need your energy."

I knew that she was right. But I just couldn't get the images of people suffering out of my head. Taking a few more bites, I turned the television back on. The weather alert kept flashing.

I needed to see where it was going to hit. It wasn't until two hours later that a satellite image of the Philippines was broadcasted. The weather woman began explaining about the high and low pressure systems that were covering the country. As I watched, I knew where the storm was heading.

"It looks like Davao is going to get hit," I said.

My mother made the sign of the cross. "They will need our prayers."

Minda stood next to me.

"How do you know this?" she asked.

I began to explain how the upper atmosphere works and how low and high pressure were the steering currents that control the storm.

At one a.m. in the morning, my eyes were still on the television, watching for updates. My mother walked to where I was sitting.

"It's late. You are not going to change what is happening. Come to bed and sleep on it. Tomorrow is another day," she said. As she was walking away, I heard her say, "I hope it doesn't come this way."

Lying in my bed, I tried shutting my eyes. But I just couldn't sleep. My mind was playing horrible scenes of people being injured or having their homes destroyed. Minda rolled over in her bed, watching me. She watched me shake my head back and forth.

A tear formed in her eyes. "Oh Ali, I wish I could help you," she said and finally rolled over and fell asleep.

The next morning, I could hear the television on. Stumbling into our front room, I saw the weather map being displayed. My thoughts were correct. The storm's outer wall was just beginning to make landfall. My mother and Minda saw me.

My mother had a smile on her face. "Good morning sleepy head," she said.

Thinking out loud, I said, "I could sure use a cup of coffee." When I began pouring myself a cup, my cell phone rang. It was Neala.

"Ali, I'm at your front door," she said.

"Be right there."

Standing next to her were two well-dressed young men. "May we come in?" she asked. I looked at her with confusion.

"Oh sure. Where are my manners? I was just going to pour some coffee. Anybody want some?"

Neala put a document in her case. "That would be nice," she said.

"How about your friends?" I asked.

Both gentlemen spoke with a Russian accent. "Yes please," they said. The smaller of the two stared at me.

Taking a drink of my coffee, I returned the stare. "Do I know you? Haven't we met before?" I said, trying to place his face.

"We have, in Tokyo, at the Battle of the Minds."

"Oh my! You are the person that I had to compete with at the finals."

"Yes, I'm the one. My name is Victor Petrov. And this is my friend Mr. Alyosha. The reason that I am here is to talk to you and tell you that I did not expect to win. If I would have gone first, I would not be here now. I caught the dialect change."

"Well, it's over and we cannot change what has happened," I said.

Victor responded, "I know, but we can change the future. And that is why I am here. To make things right."

"What do you mean?"

Neala stepped in, "Ali, what Victor is trying to say is…I know Victor's father. You know I was in Russia, a few weeks ago, right?."

"I remember."

"Well, Victor's father is the person I was visiting. He knew about you, but I did not know Victor was his son. I still didn't put the two together until after the contest was over. I have just returned from Russia and I brought Victor back with me."

Victor turned to face me. "Ali, I just want to let you know that I am giving you half of the prize money from the contest."

"My family is very well off in Russia and after Neala told me about your goal to help your fellow countrymen, I had to help. I am doing similar things in my own country. I know the money was supposed to help you start a business. So, I am presenting you with a check for five-million US dollars. I hope you will accept my offer. And who knows, someday we may to do business together," he said with a smile.

Minda stood beside me. My mother seemed shocked to see a check with so many zeros on it. Minda's eyes were the size of duck eggs. A check for five million US dollars laid in my hands.

Minda squealed. "May I hold it? I have never seen something like this before!" She kept mumbling as I laid the beautiful piece of paper in her small hands.

Victor asked me again, "Ali, would you accept my offer?"

I could see a smile on Neala's face as she looked at me. "It would start your company and make things move forward." I sighed,

"It would." I turned toward the television. A new weather update was airing. Typhoon Carlos was making landfall in Davao.

"I thought so," I mumbled.

Victor noticed me. "You care for your fellow Filipinos as much as I care for my own countrymen."

Rubbing my hands together. I looked up at him. "I accept. I have to try to help however I can."

"Good. Take it to your bank and make a deposit."

Neala looked at me. "It may take up to thirty days for the check to clear. Ali, we will also have to notify the government on this gift. It is the law."

"I know."

"After all of that, we can start to build your company. You will need a board of directors, a CEO, and a president."

I looked into Victor's eyes. "Thank you so much for doing this. I am at a loss for words."

Victor smiled at me. "You're welcome."

I was so excited about the future. "May we make a toast to mark this special occasion?" I asked.

Victor picked up his cup. "I would like that a lot," he said.

Holding our coffee cups into the air, Victor spoke. "To Tibea! All she wanted to do was make a difference and now it is time for us to try to make a difference in this world."

"To Tibea," I said, holding my coffee cup against his. But I was puzzled. "How did you know Tibea?" I asked.

"I had just left the school when you were to arrive several weeks later. I had Tibea in some of my classes and we were close friends. When I found out that she had been killed, it changed me forever."

"If I can make a difference in my own country, I hope you can here as well."

"I am sure going to try. And who knows, we might be able to do business."

Victor watched me. "What are you going to do to help?"

"I have invented a product that a typhoon cannot destroy."

Choking on his coffee, Victor said, "You have done what?"

"My compound strengthens concrete by a very large margin. Winds from the typhoons cannot rip it apart. It will save countless lives from flying debris."

"I see. We don't have typhoons in Russia, but we have flash floods, tornados, and avalanches. And everything else that Mother Nature can throw at us. After you get everything set and you're in production, give me a call," he said.

Shaking his hand, I said, "That sounds good. Thank you again."

Neala walked Victor and his companion towards the front door.

"Ali, after I take them back to the airport, I will return, and we can work on the next step. Do not say anything to anyone about this."

Smiling, I said, "I won't." I gave her a hug and whispered, "Thank you."

After several hours, Neala was back at my door. The four of us sat at the kitchen table to discuss what steps needed to be taken and in what order. I noticed Minda wanting to participate.

"Minda, could you take notes on this meeting?" My mother retrieved a paper tablet and a pencil and handed them to Minda.

Neala started off. "We need to set up an account at a local bank. Have any preferences?"

I had never thought about any local banks. This was all new to me. "No, not at all," I said.

"We can go over to the First Bank of the Philippines. They are close to us and can handle our business. You are going to have to have a name for your company. They will draw up the papers and contact the government on the taxes that will have to be paid out of the five million. We will also need to go to City Hall and get everything set up with them as well."

"Neala, I have thought of a company name that probably does

not exist yet."

"What name are you considering?" she asked, intrigued.

"I want to call it ANM Industries. It stands for Ali, Neala, and Minda. None of this would be possible if it wasn't for you and Minda."

My mother liked my answer. "Amen to that," she said.

I could tell Minda liked the idea. Her name would be part of a business.

The four of us got into Neala's SUV to head to City Hall. The clerk handed me the papers to fill out, forming the company of ANM Industries of Bacacay, Philippines.

My mother seemed excited as she signed the documents stating that she was my legal guardian. I put my name next to hers and Neala witnessed the signing of the papers. I paid the clerk the filing fees and she handed me the documents to start my company.

The clerk knew who I was. "Ali, you go out and make a difference," she said.

I looked up at her and smiled. "I am planning on doing just that." I thanked her for her help.

On our drive over to the bank, I turned sideways in my seat. "I am thinking of a board of directors. I am going to be the CEO and daddy will be the president of the company. Neala, would you be a board member and head of security?"

"I would like that a lot."

"Momma, would you be on the board? You can do whatever job you would like," I said.

She stayed quiet for several moments. "I just want to be your mother."

"I like that."

"Minda, would you be another board member? And if you want to do a job, just let me know, so I won't put someone else in that position."

"I will think about it," she said.

"Fair enough," I replied.

Entering the bank, I walked up to a desk where a nicely dressed lady was looking at her computer screen.

"May I help you?"

"I would like to open up a business account."

The woman seemed amused at first that a child wanted to open an account.

"I see," she said, giving me a mocking glance. "What kind of a business account are you looking for?"

"I am starting up a company. It will be named ANM Industries."

"I see," she said, looking at my mother and Neala. "Is she for real? I am not used to having a child in our bank wanting to open up a business account."

My mother looked at her with a serious expression. "She is dead serious about this. If you cannot help, I know of several other banking institutions that would love to take on a five-million-dollar company."

This secretary's jaw dropped. Composing herself, she asked, "Did you say a five-million-dollar business?"

"That's just the start. You have about sixty seconds to talk to me or we walk."

The bank manager, Mr. Reyes, couldn't help overhearing our conversation. "I am so sorry that you are having some problems here. May I be of service?" he said, walking toward us.

"I have a five-million-dollar check in my hands, and I want to open up a business account. If your bank cannot handle my business, I can go elsewhere."

"No, don't do that. We most certainly can work with you. May I see your check?" I pulled it out of my case. "It's written from a Russian bank," he said.

I looked up at him. "I know. It may take several weeks to clear."

"Before we can open up this account, this check must be

verified as legitimate. If it passes and we are able to clear it, then we can proceed with your account. Do you understand?"

"I understand perfectly."

"Mrs. Santana, please get me the papers that we will need to proceed."

Moments later, the secretary returned with the documents. The bank manager watched me. "Take these and fill them out entirely. How can I reach you to let you know about the check?"

I gave him my number.

"Excuse me for being rude, I do not intend to be, but what is your name?"

With my best smile, I said, "My name is Ali Cruz. I believe my name is on the front of the check and here is my passport if you need some form of identification."

"Yes, I will need to see your papers. What are your plans for your business?"

"I already have a building."

The bank manager was curious. "Where is this place?"

"It's south of town, just a few kilometers from here. It used to be Bondoc Concrete."

"I remember that place. We used to handle the account there."

"Well, Dr. Montoya has donated it to me to start my business."

"He did? Well that was very nice of him. So, what is your business going to be?"

"I am going to make a substance, that when mixed with concrete, will be able to withstand typhoon winds over four-hundred-kilometers per hour."

"That has never been done before."

"I know. That's why I invented it. And it has already been tested."

The manager shook my hand. "I will call you, just as soon I know about the check."

*****

Waiting to hear from the bank became frustrating. I tried to keep busy working with Minda and her studies, but I had so many thoughts racing through my head. I needed to make an outline of everything that I would need to get started. The first priority would be to get the electricity turned on in the building.

Next, I would need to hire some workers to clean it up, maybe do a little painting, and mow the grass around the place. Then, we would need furniture: tables, desks, computers, lamps, etc.

Then, I would need equipment to make the compound. "I think I will call it LCS, which stands for Lava Controlled Substance," I said aloud to myself. Next, we'd be making the product, and getting it out to the market. Demonstrations would have to be conducted in order to show what it can do. There was a lot of work ahead of me. I never dreamed of what it would take to start of business from scratch.

I contacted my father to let him know that I was about to start my company.

"Keep me posted," he said.

"Oh, by the way, you will be the president of AMN Industries."

"President? I like the sound of that."

"I will call you soon."

On the eleventh day of pacing the floors, I began chewing on my fingernails; a bad habit to start. I couldn't help it though. My phone rang. It was Mr. Reyes from the bank.

"Ali, I have good news. The check has cleared, and the funds are here. When can you and your mother come and sign the papers?"

"We can be there this morning."

"That will be fine. See you then."

My mother seemed calm, but I think that it is just a ruse. Minda, on the other hand, was freaking out.

"That's good," she kept saying. "You are now a millionaire."

"I never thought about it that way, but I guess I am for a little while." We both giggled.

My mother overheard our conversation. Speaking in a low voice, she said, "My Ali, at the age of five, is now a multimillionaire." She started mumbling again about this and that as she shut the front door.

Minda ran off down the road trying to hail a jeepney to take us to the bank. The three of us sat quietly on one of the benches inside. It was packed with people and a couple of cages of chickens. Minda leaned over to get a closer look at the rooster. Turning her head, she looked at me and asked, "What's next?"

"We will just have to wait. We need to get everyone together and have a meeting. Plans will have to be made."

"Am I included in these plans?"

"Most certainly. You are on the Board of Directors."

-

- Chapter Twenty-Four -

Our meeting with the bank manager went well. An account was set up so that I could make withdrawals to buy the things that were needed to get the business started. Leaving the bank, we headed over to the electric company. I opened an account to have the electricity turned on at the building. I got the same treatment as I did at the bank. Everyone looked at me strangely. My mother looked down at me with her lip tilted upwards. I explained what I needed. We signed documents from the electric company. The water and sewer system came next, along with trash pickup. After many hours of doing a lot of small things, I was tired of all the running around.

"Let's go home," I said. My mother couldn't have agreed more. "Tomorrow, we'll go over to the building and hopefully the electricity will be on. Then, we can set about hiring some workers to get the place cleaned up."

My mother liked the idea and nodded as she rubbed her tired feet.

The next morning, we were in need of cleaning supplies. Before heading over to our new building, our first stop was at GM Hardware. We picked up a couple of buckets, brushes, cleaners, and bathroom tissue. After a quick walk through, I found a variety of other items I needed. While I paid for the things at the store, Minda stepped out to flag down a jeepney. As she gave the driver the address, he wondered what we were doing at an empty building.

Exiting out the rear of the jeepney, I walked around to the driver side.

"Know of anybody who would like to work for a few days to start?"

"Doing what?"

"I own this building now and I need to get it cleaned up and have the grass mowed. I am also going to need many workers for all kinds of projects."

"I know of several people who need a job," he said.

"Can you send them my way? I will pay you for your services of bringing them here and taking them home in the afternoon."

"I can do that."

"Great. We will be working six days a week. And transportation will be very important to me."

"Okay. I will return in about two hours."

"Sounds good."

With key in hand, I opened up the gate. "Momma, let's take a selfie of us standing in front of our new building," I said with excitement. The three of us gathered together and I snapped the picture.

"Minda, would you do the honors of opening the doors of ANM Industries for the first time?" I handed her the keys. She smiled brightly at the thought.

"I would love to."

My mother squeezed my shoulders. "Ali, your heart is as big as it comes. I am so proud of you."

Looking up into her eyes, I said, "Thank you momma. Thank you for being here for me."

Our list of chores was so long that I never noticed the time. There was a honking at the front of the building. The jeepney driver had kept his word.

"Say, young lady, I don't know your name," he said.

"My name is Ali Cruz."

"Ali, I have my cousins and some of their friends here. Tell them what you want to do." Everybody stood alongside of the jeepney as I began to speak.

Moving so that I could be in front of everyone, I explained,

"I need the windows cleaned. The floor needs to be swept and mopped. The restrooms need attention. And the rear bay area needs to be attended to as well. I will pay you a good wage for your services. This building is going to house a new company that I have started. I will need employees to help maintain the building. If you are wanting a good job, then we need to sit down and get some information."

The jeepney driver smiled. "Are you going to need more people?"

"I will after we get started. We will be making a cement compound here to help the Filipino people against the typhoons that plague our nation." The workers liked what they were hearing.

Turning back toward the people standing in front of me, I said, "My name is Ali Cruz. Some of you may have heard of me. I live here in Bacacay, with my parents and my best friend, Minda. I was given a gift of knowledge by our Lord and I am going to put that knowledge to use here. I want to hire employees, put people to work, and build better buildings that can withstand a super typhoon. I will grow this company to a national level. We may even go worldwide with it, once we see how things go."

Everyone clapped their hands. A young woman spoke up. "We need a job. We have families to take care of."

"I understand. That is why I want to hire from our community. The people here need the work. So, let's get some information from each of you. I want to talk to everyone here and get to know your name."

"Minda, could you start taking down their information? I need to talk to the driver."

"Sure. Everyone, please follow me," Minda said.

Returning to the jeepney driver, I said, "We will close at five on weekdays and three on Saturdays. We will open at eight every morning, except Sunday. Can you bring them here? I will put you on my payroll if that is okay with you."

He thought for a moment. "If it is guaranteed pay, then I see no problem in transporting them here."

"I will guarantee your pay."

"Then we have a deal." I reached into my pocket and gave him a little more than he expected to receive.

"You paid me too much," he said.

"No. I think it is about right."

He smiled brightly. "My wife would be happy for the extra income."

*****

Just before five, I had everyone gather around. "The jeepney driver will be here in about fifteen minutes. I have asked him to bring you here everyday except Sunday. We will start at eight in the morning and leave at five p.m. He will pick you up at seven thirty each morning."

"I will pay you every day," I said, handing them their money.

"This will at least put some money in your pockets. We will start a weekly payroll after a couple of weeks. Is this okay with everyone?"

An older woman spoke up. "I don't know if I speak for everyone, but the money today is greatly needed and appreciated." Everyone else nodded.

"That's what I thought too. My family is in the same situation as everyone else. I don't get to see my father much. He works out of town and maybe once a month we get to see each other. This company is local and your families are the most important part of your life. After we get started making a product and shipping it out, we may have to hire some more people. A lot has been accomplished today.

We will continue on the clean up tomorrow." Looking out the

front window, I saw the jeepney pull up the front of the building. "Okay everyone, your ride is here. I hope to see your smiling faces tomorrow."

After everyone left, my mother, who seemed to have disappeared for the day, responded. "Not too bad for your first day on the job," she said.

"Thanks momma. I've never done anything like this so I just kind of winged it."

"You did. The workers liked what you said. They will go home and tell their family and friends what they did today. They will be back tomorrow. I would bet on it."

"I guess it was a pretty great day. Only one problem left that I can see." My mother was finishing up on some left-over trash. She looked over at me.

"What's that?" "We don't have a way home. Our ride left with the workers."

After pondering this for a moment, we broke out into laughter. Momma paused, "That felt good. Laughing, I mean. It's been a very long time."

"You're right momma, it does feel good."

Minda turned the lock on the front door. Stuffing the building key into her pocket, she said,

"It's not too far. Maybe three-kilometers." Standing outside of the property, Minda closed and locked the gate.

My mother made a comment. "I used to walk that far every day to go to school."

"Momma, you never told me about your childhood," I said. "Where you grew up and where your parents are now... I would love to hear your story."

She looked straight ahead as we kept walking. "I knew one day you would be asking these questions. Just didn't know it would be this soon in your life." She said and took a breath.

"Well, I grew up in a small village about fifty-kilometers from Manila. Both of my parents were killed by a typhoon that caused massive flooding. I was maybe seven at the time. My father rescued me from the flood waters, but in the process of saving me, he lost his life. I was devastated. I had no brothers or sisters to turn to. I was taken in by an aunt that I had never met before. I stayed with her until I was sixteen, but then I decided to move to Manila to try to find work so I could be on my own. That's when I met your father. Now you know about my life."

"Momma, I didn't know about your parents. I would have liked to have met my grandparents."

"You would have liked them. You have a soft heart, like they did. My father helped many family members and neighbors as well when problems arose."

"Sounds like I would have loved them," I said as my mother put her arm around my shoulder.

"You would have."

Just as we entered our front gate, a rain cloud decided to open up on us. We raced to get under the front overhang. Minda jested, "We made it just in time."

*****

Opening the front door, I saw my father standing just inside the entry.

"Daddy! You're home." I ran to him and gave him a big hug.

"Hello Ali. How have you been?" My mother hugged him and gave him a kiss.

"Hello Minda," he said, giving her a hug as well.

Sitting on our sofa, I turned to look at him. "We opened ANM Industries this morning."

With curious eyes, he said, "You did what?"

"I was given a check for five-million US dollars from the boy that I lost to in Tokyo."

My father was taken back by the news.

"Let me sit down. I need to hear this whole story," he said with amazement.

My mother's voice could be heard from the kitchen. "Do any of you want coffee?" We all accepted the offer.

I began to explain, in detail, everything that had happened since he had left for work.

"We left this morning and are now just returning. It has been a long day," I said.

Minda got up from beside me. She headed towards the kitchen to see if she and my mother could put together something to make a meal. One hour later, dinner was placed on the table, including fish, rice, and Bok-choy soup.

"This is wonderful. We had a marvelous day, and a good meal at home," I said happily. After eating, I cleaned up the kitchen. I dried the dishes and my dad put them away.

My father seemed to be impressed with me. "Well Ali… I mean, Miss-Business-Woman, what are you plans for tomorrow?"

"I have been thinking about that. We are in need of furniture, computers, a telephone system, air-conditioning, and we need to get the grass cut. I think there will be a lot more, but this will get us started," I said. I thought a moment and continued. "If you can come along, maybe give me some ideas on what we still need. Oh, and I did come up with a big problem: transportation. We had to walk home today. There are no padyaks or trikes that come out that way. I have a jeepney driver delivering the workers to and from the building."

He gave me a curious look. "You have workers?"

"Oh yes, I forgot to tell you! I hired eight people to help clean up the building."

The next morning, we arrived early. I wanted my father to get a picture of what I was trying to do.

"How many offices are in the building?" he asked.

"There are four. One for you, Neala, Minda, and myself. If Minda does not want an office, we can use it for a copy room. There is so much to do before we can even begin to think about making or shipping out any product." Walking out towards the back of the building, another building was sitting off to the side. "Let's check out that building over there," I said curiously. Opening it, we discovered an assortment of mixers nd a variety of concrete tools.

My father liked what he saw. "Now these will come in handy. They will help in getting your compound mixed."

Just after the workers arrived, I put them back on their cleaning duties. With my head buried into my cell phone, I tried to find companies that could handle our initial needs. Neala walked into the front door.

"Hello everyone."

"Neala!" I shouted, as I sprang towards her. I hugged her tightly. "I missed you."

"I see that you have been a very busy lady," she observed with a smile.

"Yes, I have. Things are starting to move forward."

"So, what has been happening since I've been away?"

"Well, we moved in yesterday morning. I hired eight workers to help in cleaning the place up. We still need to have the grass cut and the air conditioning needs to be repaired or replaced. We need desk, chairs, computers, and lamps. Oh, I am going to need a rock crusher like the one we used in Cebu," I explained, then continued with my list.

"We can use the tower in the back to store the mixture. We are going to need some sort of a sack to put the mixture in so we can carry it to the different places we sell to. We are also in need of transportation for my family and myself. We either have to walk to work or try to catch a jeepney." I took a breath. We have so much to do. "Then, we will be needing to bring the lava here. It will have to be picked up with a dozer or backhoe or something like that."

Neala looked around. "Okay. Let's make a list of everything you just said."

"I already have. I was looking on my cell phone for furniture places when you arrived."

"Any luck?"

"A few in Legaspi City."

"Okay then. We need to make a trip."

"Dad, Neala and I are going shopping for some furniture and maybe some computers. Can you hold down the fort until we can return? We will bring back lunch for everyone as well."

"Go ahead. We can handle anything here."

"Oh, can you try to find someone who can look at the air conditioning unit? It would be a great help."

"I will look into it."

*****

A stop at Furniture Giant was unsuccessful. I was not comfortable with the salesman. He kept hitting on Neala and was not focusing on helping me with purchasing furniture.

After about ten seconds of putting up with him, I had to bark out my thoughts. "Let's go. There are other places I want to check out." A small furniture store on a back street of Bacacay didn't look too promising either.

Sitting in the parking lot, Neala put her car into reverse and said, "No. Let's at least give it a try. We can always walk away," I said. Stepping inside, we were amazed at all the furniture that was inside the building.

An older man with wire rimmed glasses came up to Neala.

"May I help you dear?" he asked. Neala pointed at me. "She is the one who needs furniture."

I began to explain what I needed. I saw him smile as I asked about desks, chairs, and lamps. He took us to another part of this building that had nothing but office furniture.

"Now we're talking." I picked out four desks, with chairs. "Let's hold off on the lamps for now. We are in need of a kitchen table to put in the break room with chairs. And I almost forgot. We are going to need a microwave and a stove top to cook on. And the last thing that I can think of would be a refrigerator. Walking over to where the gentleman stood, I looked up at him. "How much will these items cost? And can you deliver to this address?" He looked at what I had picked out.

"How do you wish to pay my dear?"

"Do you take plastic?"

With a big smile on his face, he said, "I sure do."

Neala pulled out our check list. After marking off a large portion of things needed, she commented, "Computers are next on the list."

"I saw an ad on the television yesterday. The Computer Room has some on sell this week."

Let's go check them out."

As we entered, a very nice saleswoman walked up to Neala. "May I be of assistance?" Neala pointed in my direction.

"Someday I will be tall enough to be asked if they can help me instead of the adults," I thought to myself. While looking around, I had my eye on a laptop computer. After she gave me her sales pitch, I chose four high-end laptops. With computers in our hands, Neala and I headed to her SUV.

Neala started the engine. "What's next?"

I rubbed my stomach. "Lunch."

"Now that sounds wonderful," she said. We ate a delicious meal until we were stuffed.

With a to-go order for everyone at work, it was time to head back. On the drive back to the office I noticed several automobile dealerships.

"We still need to find some kind of transportation. I like riding with you, but you know...." She gave me a curious look. We both laughed at my joke.

*****

Back at the office, everyone was fed and Neala and I unloaded the computers.

"We have furniture coming tomorrow. In the meantime, we will have to sit on the floor."

After my father finished his lunch, he looked at me. "I made some calls to several air conditioning companies. And I have one coming this afternoon. I hope that it is okay with you," he said.

"Oh yes. With the outside temperature reaching the thirty-six degree Celsius mark, air conditioning would be a blessing."

One of the workers spoke up. "My cousin has a lawn mower and is looking for work. Would you like to talk to him about cutting the grass here?"

"Oh, please. That would be great. Have him come here tomorrow," I said.

"I will tell him."

"Dad, we are in need of transportation," I said with a straight face, looking into his eyes.

"Do you know how to drive?" I asked. He grabbed his wallet and removed his driver's license to show it to me.

"I was driving long before you were born."

"That's fantastic. We are in need of a car, van or something that can take us to work and around. Neala has been so helpful, but she has other things that she has to attend to."

After the workers had left, and it was time to return home, we all piled into Neala's car. That was a sight. Five of us piled into a four-seater. My dad had his head out the window just so he could breathe. Pulling up to the front of our house, his first words were, "Yep we are definitely in need of a bigger vehicle." while everyone climbed out of Neala's SUV. She waved over the roof and yelled, "Later!"

The next morning, Neala was waiting patiently outside. Once again, the four of us climbed into her small SUV, and my father jokingly said, "Here we go again!" My parents were both in agreement on the car situation.

My mother could not move in the back seat. "Let's open up the building and then we are going car shopping," she said.

"Sounds good to me."

*****

Pulling up to the front gate, I could see everyone had arrived and were eager to put in a full day of work. "Okay everybody, we are having some furniture delivered today. There will be a kitchen table and chairs, a microwave oven, a small stove top and a refrigerator."

They cheered. "We will be able to cook lunch!"

"Minda, would you stay here and wait for the furniture to arrive? And also, there will be a man with a lawnmower to cut the grass. Here is some money to pay him.

You can also pick out what office you want because I bought you a desk and chair. Then you can work on getting your computer up and running. I will have to check into getting internet service as well." She nodded.

"I never realized how much there is to do to start a business," I said.

My father agreed and added, "But in the long run, you are

your own boss. You work hard, make a living for yourself or your family. And one day you will get to retire. And that is how it is supposed to go."

Pulling away from the front of the building, we had all the windows rolled down. It seemed my father had developed a gas problem. One of the workers saw us. She told the others to look and chuckled, "Now that's funny. They all have their heads hanging out the windows of that car!"

My father didn't know that he taken on as an adversary with his "issue."

Neala made a comment in a low voice. "Just you wait. Payback time will come." We all laughed while heading down the street.

After making several stops at different dealerships, I settled on a Toyota SUV that could hold all of us and had enough room in the rear to put things in. A salesman came out of his office to talk to us. "Would you like to test drive this fine automobile?" he asked. My father looked down at me.

"All I am saying is that you're the driver. That is your decision," I said. The salesman looked at us funny.

He couldn't figure out why my father was asking a child if it was okay for him to test drive this SUV. My mother and Neala were snickering when they left.

"I know... Get used to it," I said, repeating what I had been told so many times.

After a thirty minute wait, I began pacing the floor of the dealership. "Where can they be? We have things to do today." I caught sight of my father and the salesman slapping each other on the back.

Walking over to where they were standing, I asked, "Is everything okay?"

"Everything is great. Ali, Mr. Larkin and I went to the same school. We spoke once at a soccer game."

"I see. So, dad, can we wrap up our business here? I have to get back to the office."

Mr. Larkin scratched the back of his head. Looking at my father, he asked, "Is she your boss?"

"Yep, and a darn good one too."

"Since you two are buddies and all, do we get a discount?" I asked, going into my 'business mode.'

Mr. Larkin studied me for a moment. "Let me check with my boss."

Returning to his office, he handed me a piece of paper with a price for the SUV.

"Now, is this the drive-off price?"

He looked at me. "It is."

"Good. I will take it."

"How do you wish to pay?"

"It will be on my credit card." I caught the smirk look on his face when I handed him my card.

"I'll be right back. I will have to run your card through your bank." Five minutes had passed when he returned.

The salesman looked at me quizzically. "As soon as I gave the woman at your bank the account numbers, she asked who was using your card," he said.

"When I told her, all she said was to let you buy whatever you wanted. Let's fill out the paperwork and get a few signatures." An hour later, our business was concluded. I had just purchased a new SUV. Neala headed out the door.

"Later," she said, waving her arms as she left. Sitting in the back of the vehicle, I noticed the new car smell.

"I like the smell," I observed.

*****

Pulling into the yard of the office, all the windows were down. A worker saw us with our heads sticking out the sides. "Not again," he laughed.

The furniture had arrived before we returned from car shopping. Minda had chose a small office off to the right side of the building for herself.

"Not sure what I am going to be doing here," she stated.

"Well, for starters, you can work on payroll, expenses, and that sort of thing. In general, do the accounting of the company."

She looked at me. "I like it. I guess the education that I have been getting will come in handy after all."

"It will."

My mother looked at Minda. "Can you handle a big job like this?" she asked. Minda glanced at the floor.

With an upbeat voice, she answered, "I sure can."

I gave her a high-five. "Good. Then, it's settled. We will also continue your education. It seems you like numbers, so we will work harder in that field."

Minda was quiet for a moment. I caught the words she spoke in a muffled voice. "Thanks Ali, for everything."

- Chapter Twenty-Five -

Our new building was progressing nicely. The air conditioning system was shot and had to be replaced. The buildings electrical system was in need of updates. A new rock crusher used to grind up the lava was installed, along with a large water tank to hold the sea water. I made a call to the Department of the Interior to get the necessary permits so I could retrieve the lava from all of the volcanoes in the Philippines. Once we had the shop up and running, we would to have to expand to other areas of the country. But that plan was for the future. For the time being, I needed to have the lava brought here. I contacted Neala. After I explained to her what I needed, she was able to find a trucking company that would load up the lava and have it delivered.

*****

Minda had just opened the doors to the building when several large dump trucks rolled into the yard. Neala was waving from the passenger side of the first truck.

"Where do you want it?" she called. I climbed up on the running board, and I yelled, "Head towards the rear of the property and drop the loads near the conveyors."

"This is good," I yelled to the driver. After they dropped their loads, Neala climbed back in the first truck. "I'll be back later."

I waved at her. "Okay."

Looking at everything I had before me, I knew something was missing. My dad walked to where I was standing.

"How are you going to get the lava up and into the grinder?" he chuckled and left.

Some kind of dozer or backhoe was needed for this job. I waited for Neala to return.

"Do you know anything about heavy equipment?"

"Not really."

"This will be my next problem to solve." After a few calls were made, a small backhoe-like machine was delivered.

I asked the workers if anyone had experience working with that type of machinery. A small, petite woman who was with the clean-up crew spoke up. "I can work this machine. I have on several occasions worked with my brother on his."

She stood next to it. "May I?"

"Oh, please do," I said, moving out of her way. She put on a hard hat and eye protection. Then she climbed into the backhoe and fired up its engine. Moving the machine over to the lava pile, she scooped up a bucket full. Taking it to the conveyor belt, she dropped the load onto it. Dawning a hard hat and eye protection, I stopped everyone from doing any job in the work bay area.

"Everyone who steps outside here from now on will have to have eye protection as well as a hard hat. This is mandatory. We do not need to have you injured or hurt because of something that could have been prevented," I announced.

I started up the rock crusher. The noise from the lava being crushed was horrendous. "We are in need of hearing protection as well. This noise level is just too high to be near," I said.

Neala left. Two hours later, she returned with earmuffs and ear plugs. She also bought breathing masks as well.

"Good thinking. This will work." Dawning the safety equipment, everyone headed outside to see how we were going to start this business. With the crusher running again, the lava was pulverized into fine particles. Then, a conveyor belt took the product over to the water to be soaked. Once the mixture had dried into a dust-like substance, it would be mixed with the concrete cement. "The lava will have to sit in a holding container until it can dry," I explained.

The following morning, I tested the lava sand. It was dry enough to make the mixture. I saw Neala standing next to someone that I did not know. I pointed at the door. "Let's go inside to talk."

"Ali, this is Maria Bonzagales. She is with Channel Four News. I have explained to her about what is about to happen here and I think this would be good for business."

I introduced myself to Maria and explained what we were doing. Her camera man turned on his camera.

"Now if you go into the yard, everyone must put on safety attire," I said.

We all put on the safety equipment as instructed. Everybody watched as I joined the lava and the cement. As I poured it into a bag, pictures were taken of this historical event. Standing next to my dream, I started to cry. Between sobs I stated, "Today, we are making history. This product will change the lives of everyone in the Philippines." Everyone clapped.

"We are now in business," I proudly announced. Channel Four News wanted to do an interview. To explain what was going on, I retrieved my laptop and played the film that was taken at Caplin Mining of my wall verses the ordinary one.

After seeing the results, the reporter stated, "You are on to something big. May I have a copy of the wall video?"

"Sure," I said, giving her a copy on a flash drive.

That evening, while Minda and my mother were cooking up dinner, my father and I were sitting on the sofa watching the six o'clock news. "Change it to channel four." He grabbed the remote and flipped the channel.

Several minutes had gone by. I wondered if we missed it.

"Now with breaking news. A special report from Maria Bonzagales. We are in the midst of seeing history being made. Do you remember the young girl named Ali Cruz who shocked the nation with her extremely high IQ? Well, she has done it again."

The television switched from my interview, to the video of my wall experiment. They returned back to the reporter. "She is planning to market this new compound all over the Philippines. What will this mean for the people? A safer place to live. No more collapsing walls caused by typhoons. Stronger buildings in the cities. Nothing like this has ever been invented before."

The news anchor came back on. "Her new company, ANM Industries, is located in Bacacay."

My father patted my arm. "Is this what you wanted?'

"It is, Daddy. The people will be able to have a chance against these storms."

"I think you are right. What are your plans now?"

"We wait. This story should go viral across the country, and maybe worldwide. If so, we are going to be growing at a tremendous rate."

I was right. The next morning, my phone was ringing non-stop. Building contractors from around the country wanted in on my new product. They were asking for ten-thousand bags, then twenty-thousand.

"What kind of delivery time is expected?" they'd ask. I became overwhelmed with questions.

My father looked over his shoulder from the front seat.

He caught the expression I had on my face. "Well, I am in need of your help here."

He laughed. "You should see the look on your face."

"What look? We just went from no business to one of the top in the country. We are needing to fill a lot of product." On the way to the office, I took a minimum of twelve more calls, jotting down notes on each caller, and how much product they needed.

A meeting was called for all the employees. My father began to speak, "Since our news debut yesterday, we have become an overnight sensation. Our product is in need all over the country. In order to meet these demands, this company will go into full production. That means we will be running a shift around the clock, seven days a week. Therefore, we will have to hire a lot more workers. We will need people to run the dozer, fill the bags, take our product to markets, and run the office when we are not here. If you know of anyone who would like a job, and can do this type of work, please send them our way."

Word of mouth about us hiring spread like wildfire. We had nearly two-hundred people at the front of the building the next morning. Each was given a form to fill out. The ones that could not read or write were given verbal questions. Something I would never do was not give somebody a chance who wanted to better themselves.

The interviewing took another five days to get the people hired and trained on running the equipment and the office. Looking over the roster of ANM Industries, we now had fifty-three people on our payroll.

Standing next to me, my father stared out the large picture window.

"We have approximately three-thousand bags filled by the third week of operations."

I knew what my father was talking about. "This is good, but we are going to have to expand our plant's operations in order to fill our orders."

My father watched the work being performed. "They are working at a vigorous pace, but we are not even getting close to filling up the orders."

I looked up at him. "The property that our building is residing on could hold one more crusher and another set of holding bins. We would also need another water tank for the sea water and the concrete cement. After looking over our expenditures, it seems we have currently spent approximately one-point-nine-million dollars."

"It will cost around eight-hundred-thousand to buy the extra equipment. We have sold, at the close of business today, three-thousand bags of compound. We now have orders for approximately eighty-six thousand more bags. And the list is getting longer."

My father removed his eyeglasses from his face. "I know. I have already ordered the new equipment."

I smiled at him. "Good."

- Chapter Twenty-Six -

AMN Industries was still not making enough product to satisfy all of our clients. I had to hire an additional twenty-three employees to make up ground on the production side. A board meeting was called to see what could be done to meet the demand. With everyone seated, my father began, "I am looking at buying more land somewhere around several volcanoes. I want to open additional offices at different locations. Ever since the news story broke about AMN Industries, we have been overwhelmed by consumers. We have already expanded here once." I sat there, listening to the business side of our company.

I stood up from the table. "We could outsource our compound to Caplin Mining. They, of course, would get a portion of the profits to cover their cost."

My father looked towards Minda. "What's our profit margin?"

"We are at twenty-eight percent. It would cut a small percentage, but we could go three percent," she said.

My father looked at everyone. "I have been receiving emails from investors who would like to invest in our company. The one that is high on my list is Dr. Montoya. He has sent me several emails and has asked that I return a message," he said.

I stood up in front of the group. "There is a lot to consider here. First, do we expand to meet our client's needs? Second, do we go to outside sources to try to make up differences in our product volume? And third, do we take on investors to help with financing our expansion of the company to other provinces?"

My father looked at everyone seated. "Since this company just started a few months ago, we have had to expand to try to satisfy our customers. At the current rate of production, we are not even close to filling our orders. That is why I called this meeting."

Neala jumped into the conversation. "We are going to have to do everything possible, not just pick one or the other. If we cannot meet the customer's needs, then we go under in a very short time. No company has ever mae a difference by sitting back and not listening to its customers."

I looked at Neala and whispered, "I see Tibea in your heart."

She smiled. "I am learning a lot, being around you." I smiled back gracefully at her.

"I will respond to Dr. Montoya's email and set up a meeting. And something that I had thought of ever since we took over this building. I want to pay Dr. Montoya what he was asking for this building. I will not ever take advantage of anyone," I said. "So, can I get a vote on paying for the building?" It was a five to zero vote. "Thanks. I will also look into how Caplin Mining can relieve some of our backlog."

A meeting with Dr. Montoya was set up for three p.m., along with a video conference with Caplin Mining for Thursday at two p.m.

There was a knock on my door. Looking up, I saw Dr. Montoya standing there.

"Hello Ali."

"Hello doctor." I apologized for not being prepared. "I was just going over emails. Please come in and sit." I made a call to Minda and my father.

With everyone seated around my desk, Dr. Montoya waved his arms around. "You have done wonders for this old building. How many employees do you have on your payroll?"

Minda spoke in a professional tone. "We are at seventy-six."

Dr. Montoya looked at Minda. "Are you supposed to be in school, young lady?" he asked. Minda got a kick out of watching the doctor's facial expressions.

"I was, but I have already passed the high school exit test.

Now I am taking college courses."

"Just how old are you, may I ask?"

"I'm seven."

"And what is your job title for this company?"

"I am the paymaster and bookkeeper."

Dr. Montoya looked at me. "Did you have something to do with her education?"

I smiled politely. "You could say something like that."

The doctor smiled. "When we have finished our business, you and I need to talk about some kind of education program for the Filipinos."

Tucking my hair behind my ears, I said, "You never know what the future may hold."

Doctor Montoya liked what he heard. "Do you have any documentation on how you are doing financially?" Minda produced a folder with all the documents that he would need to look over.

"If I like the figures that I am looking at, I am willing to put two-million US dollars in AMN Industries. I will let you know by ten o'clock tomorrow morning."

"May I now see your plant operations?"

Getting up from behind my desk, I said, "You sure may." We donned the safety equipment and headed outside to the back of the building.

He watched as workers put the lava through the crushers, then the lava was soaked in water and mixed with the cement and bagged. Walking back into my office, Dr. Montoya seemed fascinated at watching everyone work so fluently. "How did you accomplish this so fast?" he asked.

"Well, for starters, I pay them more than any other job that involves similar labor.

They are happy to take home more money to their families. You can see the outcome. Also, I called a board meeting and I want to give you a check for the three-hundred-thousand pesos. That was the price you were asking for this building."

He looked at me. "I gave the building to you."

"I know you did. But I do not want to have anyone think that I am taking advantage of them. I know that you are a businessman and this matter has bothered me for a while."

I could see the side of his mouth raise. He politely replied, "Okay."

"It's nothing personal. This is just business."

He looked at me standing behind my desk. "I like the way you talk. Very professional," he said. I handed him the check and he put it away.

"I will call you tomorrow and give you my answer about the investment."

"Thank you, doctor, for coming here for this meeting."

My father walked into my office. "Well, how did it go?" he asked.

"He was impressed with our business practices. Something is still bothering me though. I know that I am forgetting something."

Then, it hit me like a brick in the head. "We do not have a corporate lawyer," I said with realization.

My father leaned against the door jam. "Exactly."

"I will give Neala a call. She may know a lawyer or two." I made the call. As I hung up the phone, I told my father, "Neala mentioned several attorneys."

After hours of phone calls, I had an attorney on the payroll.

Walking into my father's office, I announced, "I have hired an attorney. Her name is Elizabeth Cortez."

"Is she expensive?"

"Not too bad."

"Is there anything else I am forgetting to hire, buy, sell, or trade?"

My father studied my body expressions. "Everything that you have learned in books will not prepare you for working in the real world. You may have a lot of knowledge, but, as you are aware, you are only scratching the surface when it comes to making money and dealing with people, both customers and employees."

With my backside up against a wall, I said, "I know. That's right."

Just before ten a.m. the next day, my phone rang. It was Dr. Montoya.

"Ali, I have decided to invest with your company. I looked over the numbers your accountant gave me, and I think it would be good for business for both of us. Do you have an attorney that can draw up the papers?"

"I do," I said, giving him the information.

"Okay, great! I will send her the information and have the funds transferred into your account. We need to have lunch sometime. I would love to get your take on education. I am still amazed on how you taught the other girl."

"Do you mean Minda?"

"Oh yes, that is her. Fascinating how you taught her so quickly."

Minda walked into my office an hour later. "The funds just hit the bank," she said.

"Great!" I responded with enthusiasm.

"That puts us just over four million in our account," Minda said

*****

"My Father decided to take a business trip to Bulusan to check out some property there to buy. Since it is near a volcano, we could set up another office like this one." With my father gone, my mother had to take over the duties of driving our SUV. With one foot on the gas pedal and the other on the brake, she made our heads whip back and forth, like a heavy metal band at a rock concert.

"If I could reach the pedals, I could do this," I commented.

She gave me an evil stare.

I returned her gaze and shrugged. "Just saying."

"Hush," she said.

As we backed up, a horn blared at us. She pulled forward again. I turned around, "It's okay to go backwards now, Mom." She put the car in reverse, hit the brake hard, shifted into forward, and we started our journey home.

Looking around the front seat, I could see Minda with her hair covering her entire face.

"You look like something from a sci-fi movie!" I laughed.

"Mom, have you ever driven a car before?"

"No," was the answer I got.

With a polite voice, I said, "Okay then. We are going to have to download the driver's handbook."

My mother began mumbling under her breath, "Driver's handbook, "Hum."

After dinner, I loaded up several videos on basic driving and a copy of the driver's handbook on my on my laptop. "Here mom. This may help you. You are going to have to get a license to be able to drive."

"I know. It's just…" Then her voice dwindled off.

While my mother began to study the rules of the road, I went to Minda. "Do you want to work on your studies?" She thought about it for a moment.

"Do you think that it will help me now?"

"If you would like to have a college degree, then yes. When clients come into your office and see your diploma, they will be more comfortable talking with you. Your self-esteem is high and you will carry yourself proudly. No one can take that away from you."

She looked down at the floor. "I wish my parents could see me now."

"I truly believe that they are watching over you. They know you are doing everything in your power to move forward and are not taking a backseat to what happened to them. They could not be any prouder of you. I know I couldn't be either."

She smiled, "Thanks Ali, for everything. I really mean it."

"I know you do."

"Okay now. So much for the mushy stuff," I said and pulled a book off the shelf. Opening it up to the calculus problems, I said, "Here, work on these. I will check your answers later."

As I turned the television on, a breaking news report was on about a Typhoon Darna that was just forming off the coast of Siargao Islands.

"Here we go again." My mother and Minda sat down near me. We watched as the information was being broadcasted.

"It's too early to tell what direction this storm will head."

My mother put one arm around me and the other around Minda. "Let's hope your father makes it back before anything bad happens."

"I hope so, Momma."

*****

The next morning, I looked for Minda but could not find her .anywhere. "Momma, have you seen Minda this morning?"

"I saw her walk outside earlier." I found her sitting on the curb, near our car.

Standing next to Minda, I asked, "What's up?" She looked up at me.

"I'm praying. Yesterday nearly killed me. I am considering cutting off all my hair. Not sure about the punk rock thing though," she let out an uneasy laugh.

"If you shave your head, you would fit right in." We both giggled.

I responded, "We made it home safely, didn't we? And I don't think it can get any worse.

"We will see. I said my Hail Mary and brought my crucifix with me." We could hear my mother closing the front door. Minda stood up. "Here she comes. Oh Lord. We are in for it now."

"Shush! You are going to make matters worse."

"You girls ready for another day?" my mother asked. Minda did her blessings, kissing her crucifix. My mother saw her.

"I didn't know that you are Catholic," my mom said. Minda gave me the eye, as she buckled herself in.

Putting the car in forward, my mother gave it too much gas. She laid two strips of black rubber in front of our house. We hadn't gone but just a few meters when she hit the brakes hard. It seemed that an older lady carrying a rooster under her arm decided to walk in front of us. Turning in my seat, I could see Minda, making a scissor effect with her right hand to her hair. Her face was totally covered, yet again, by her long beautiful black hair. Pulling into the parking lot, I knew my friend was not in a very good mood.

Walking past Neala's office, we heard her say, "Something wrong?" Minda kept walking. She went into her office and shut the door. Thirty minutes later, she walked out with a new hairstyle. She had cut off most of her hair. Neala saw her walk by. "Cute haircut," she said. As she stuck her head into my office, I just smiled. She gave me a look, then left.

The office routine was going at its normal pace when my mother walked down the hallway.

"I'm going out for lunch. Anybody want to join me?" There was no sound coming from Minda's office. Checking in on her, I saw that she had earbuds stuck in her ears. She pulled one out when

I stuck my head in her office. "My mother wants to know if you would like to go to lunch with her. She's driving." Minda raised her hands while mouthing, "No, No, No!"

"Okay, I'll tell her that you will meet her at the car." As I turned to walk out of her office, she made a crazy face over the top of the computer monitor.

"Girl, you need to go to confession!"

Turning on a small television that we kept in the break room, I wanted to check the weather report about typhoon Darna. Just past noon, a weather bulletin was posted. Typhoon Darna had just turned into a super typhoon, packing winds of over four-hundred kilometers per hour.

"This is not good." Landfall would be between Tacloban City and the Island of Panaon. Hearing the television newscast, Neala walked into the break room. "Have you heard from your father?"

"No, not a word so far. He is supposed to be back by tomorrow," I paused. "I can't watch this right now. I have too much work to do."

Later that afternoon, I received a phone call. It was my father. "Daddy? Where are you? Are you okay?"

"Everything is fine. I left Bulusan and came down to Tacloban City. I have heard that they built a storm shelter using our product. I wanted to see it firsthand and get some pictures. This would be great advertisement for us."

"Good thinking Dad, but you know a super typhoon may be headed your way. It formed late yesterday."

"I know. The airport has just shut down. I cannot leave."

"Okay, Dad. Stay safe and I will see you soon. I love you."

"I love you too."

"Dad, have you talked to mom?"

"Not yet. Can you put her on the phone?" I scrambled around the building looking for her. She was cleaning a window when I approached her.

"Momma, Dad wants to talk to you," I said, handing her the phone. I could not concentrate on business. My mind kept thinking of my father. A super typhoon was nothing to mess with. Its destructive path covers hundreds of kilometers. No one is safe if they are caught in one of these storms.

Later that evening, when we had just finished dinner, I turned on the television. Typhoon Darna had moved into Leyte Gulf. With sustained winds of over four -hundred kilometers an hour, it was now considered one of the strongest typhoons ever recorded. I watched as the weatherman pointed out the low-pressure areas in that part of the country.

I screamed, "Momma, Tacloban City is going to take a direct hit! Daddy is in the middle of this storm!"

Minda watched me. I was shaking vigorously from the thought that my father may be killed. I tried to call his phone but there was no service.

My mother patted my shoulders. I could see tears in her eyes. "This is as real as it gets. Life and death," I sobbed to myself.

I knew my mom wouldn't sleep until she could hear his voice, call his name, and hear the most comforting words of all: "I Love You." The only thing we could do was wait.

My mother sat on the end of the sofa and curled herself up closing her eyes. I could only imagine what was going through her mind. She had already lost loved ones because of these storms. Minda and I moved a little closer to her. I picked up my mother's hand. Minda did the same to her other hand.

"We are all in this together," I reassured her.

The next day, I tried to concentrate on the business. Waiting to hear about the aftermath of the storm was maddening. It was the not-knowing part that really got to me. We had no word on how the people of Tacloban City were. The weatherman stated that no one was able to get in until after the winds died down. Only then, could the rescue workers go in and check to see if everyone was okay.

At almost five p.m., I heard the television in the break room come on. Momma wanted to get a news update. A camera crew was flown in by helicopter to shoot some video of the destruction of the city. There were hundreds of buildings torn apart. Some were just gone. I ran into the room to see the video of Tacloban City. The film crew had landed near the storm shelter.

With my eyes glued to the television, I saw the main door of the shelter starting to open. There was my father standing with a little girl in his arms. My mother started crying. I too had tears in my eyes. Minda and Neala rushed into the room and stood next to us. A reporter walked up to my father. "Is anybody hurt? Is everyone okay in there?"

"Everyone is fine." I saw him looking at the older shelter that was near this new one. The camera man picked up on his gaze. A microphone was moved close to him. "That was the old shelter. It looks like it was destroyed. I am not sure if anybody went into it," he said.

"Who is this little girl you are holding?" A reporter asked, putting a microphone up to his face.

"I don't know her name. I was running towards this shelter when I saw her and her parents trying to escape from their van. When suddenly, a wall of concrete blocks hit their car. If you look over there, you can see where it happened." The cameraman panned over to the crushed van.

"I ran over to see if I could help anyone, that's when I found her. She was crying loudly, looking for her momma. I picked her up and brought her here with me. She has not let me go since. I don't think I can ever let her go."

Several medical teams landed and began to check on everyone. They took the little girl from my father's arms. I watched him break down crying.

"It's okay sir. We just want to check her out. We will return her to you in a moment."

I could hear my father tell the medic, "She needs water and food. She has not eaten in two days."

The news woman returned to the camera. "As you can see, this new kind of structure was built with a new material that can withstand the strength of a typhoon. We need more like this here and all over the Philippines."

My mother had a strange look on her face. She turned to Minda and I.

"When we get home tonight, Ali, you and Minda prepare your room for your new sister." Both of us were shocked.

"A new sister? What do you mean?"

With tears in her eyes, my mother said, "That little girl your father is holding, is another you."

"Another me? What are you talking about?"

My mother broke down into a wash of tears. Wiping her eyes on her shirt, she said, "There is something about my life that I have never told you. I was almost five months pregnant when I developed some complications. I was not going to be able to carry the full term. My baby had to be taken. I was having a very hard time with losing her. I went into depression. Your father didn't know what to do. We found out that I was not able to have children."

The bottle of water that I was holding slipped out of my hand, hitting the floor. Putting my hands up to my face, I stood motionless. "Do you mean what I think you mean? I am adopted?"

With more tears pouring out of her eyes, my mother's voice was shrilled as she said, "Yes. Father Bayon knew about the problems that we had with the pregnancy. He approached us about adopting a little girl whose parents were killed in a typhoon like this one. We thought about the adoption for a couple of months. That is when we decided to talk to Father Bayon. He took us to where this little girl of no more than nine months old was being cared for. I took one look and could not take my eyes off of her. 'I want her!' I told him. Everything was prepared and we took home the most beautiful little girl in the world. That moment when I saw you for the first time, I knew we needed you in our lives."

I covered my mouth. Tears were running down my face like rainwater.

"That little girl that you saw on the television with your father will become your sister, come hell or high water," she said.

Minda stood next to me. "We are one," she said with a nod.

I looked into her eyes. "We are."

After several more days of waiting, my father finally made it home. I knew that he and my mother were doing everything they could to adopt that little girl. Even Father Bayon was brought in to see if he could help.

*****

For the next three months, my business was growing at an astounding rate. We bought property all over the Philippines, built new buildings, and hired hundreds of workers to run the business.

My parents finally received a certified letter from the adoption agency. They were approved to adopt the little girl. My mother sat on the sofa next to me. "Ali, what are we going to call her?" she asked.

Thinking about it for a moment, I responded, "I like Maria."

My mother smiled. "I think that is an excellent name. Maria Cruz. Your father and I have to fly down and get her tomorrow."

"Can you have Neala stay here while we are away?"

"I'll ask."

Neala answered her phone on the first ring. After I explained about my parents having to make a trip, Neala told me that it was not going to be a problem for her to come stay for a few days.

Neala, Minda, and I were sitting down at our table, having dinner when something in the back of my mind kept me thinking. I need to go see Father Bayon."

She looked at me. "When?"

"Tomorrow will be okay."

*****

Arriving at the Catholic Church, I saw Father Bayon kneeling in front of Christ on the cross. Hearing me enter, he rose and walked to where I was standing. Taking his hand, I put it to my forehead. "Father, may we sit?" He led me to a pew.

"You know that I am adopted."

"Yes. I know."

"And you knew my real parents."

"Yes, I knew them."

"What can you tell me about them?"

"Well, they had just moved to our city. They were not people who came to church a lot. But they did come once in a while. I had spoken to them on several occasions about things in general. You know, life things that all young couples experience. I always saw your mother carrying a little girl in her arms every time I met with them."

My eyes were wet with tears. I looked into his eyes. "It was me, wasn't it?"

"It was. Life was going good for them, when we were suddenly hit by a typhoon. The place where they were staying… the roof caved in on them. After the storm, I was told about the tragic events. I started asking about what had happened to you. That was about the time when your mother lost her baby. I followed my heart and introduced your parents to you."

Neala and Minda were sitting in the rear pews. I could hear

sobbing noises coming from both of them.

Father Bayon looked up at me. "I understand that you are going to have a new sister in your life."

"We are. We are going to name her Maria. Father, there is something that is bothering me."

"What's that, my child?"

"Our business is doing very well and is growing at an alarming rate. But deep in my soul, I feel like something is still missing. I need to do something with all of my knowledge."

Father Bayon knew exactly what I was talking about. "You want to know why you were chosen to retain so much knowledge and what are you going to do with it. And I have always said that you already know the answer. You just haven't figured out how to bring it to the surface so you can grasp it."

"Yes Father, you are correct. The thing that I want to do more than anything in this world is to teach."

Father Bayon took off his glasses. "I was wondering when you would come forth with your answer. I knew this was what our Lord had in mind when he gave you your extraordinary mind. The day that you asked me about the books I was carrying, I knew then what I was witnessing. That was why I asked Father Castillo to see for himself. I wanted him to witness the gift that our Lord had given you. You accomplished so much in such a very short time. You said that you wanted to help your fellow Filipinos. You invented a product that has and will save many lives. You have given jobs to a lot of people so they too can make their own lives prosper. You helped your friend Minda to overcome her great loss and are giving her an education second to none. And now you want to teach others so they too may enrich their own lives. That, my child, is one of the greatest gifts that any human can bestow. I am very proud to know you."

Minda and Neala came forward and stood next to me. "Father, I would like to give thanks to everyone who believed in me."

He rose from the pew. Standing in front of the Holy Cross, he asked, "Would you ladies like to kneel with me?"

THE END

Fun facts

The
PHILIPPINES

**According to
Wikipedia**

Jeepney

A jeepney is a bus or merely a jeep that is used as a means of public transportation in the Philippines.

For more information, go to:
https://en.wikipedia.org/wiki/Jeepney

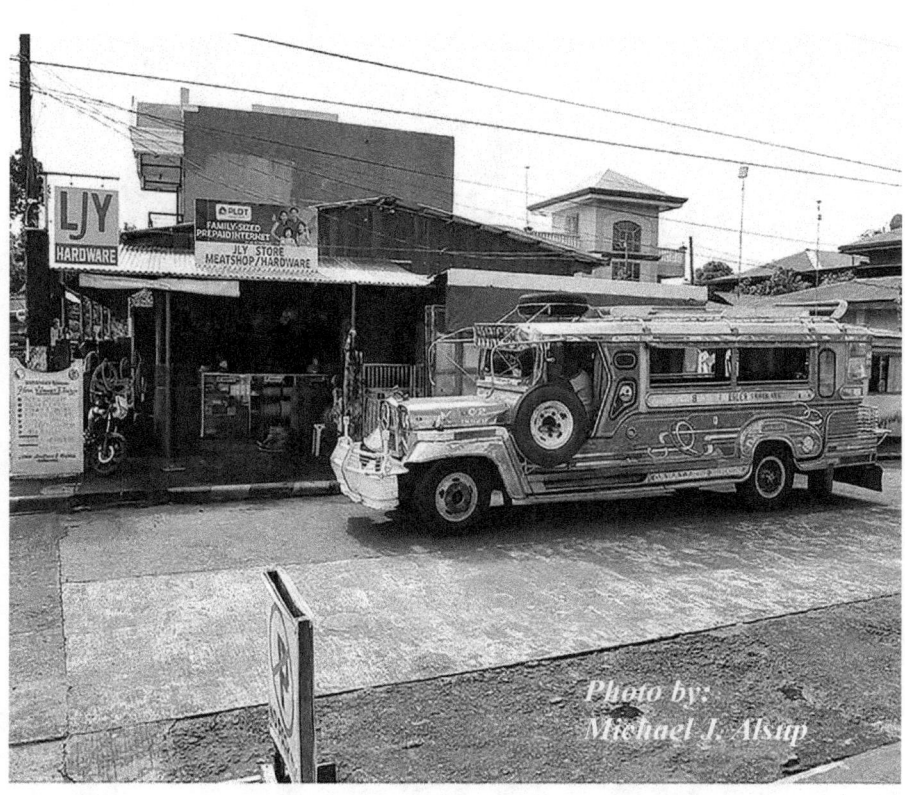

Photo by:
Michael J. Alsup

Padyak

A Philippine pedicab is called a traysikad, trisikad — or simply sikad or padyak, from the Philippine word meaning to tramp or stamp one's feet. It is made by mounting a sidecar to a regular bicycle. They are used mainly to ferry passengers short distances along smaller, more residential streets, often to or from jeepneys or other public utility vehicles. They are also used for transporting cargo too heavy to carry by hand and over a distance too short or roads too congested for motor transport, such as a live pig. During rainy seasons, they are useful as a way to avoid walking through flood waters. Along with the jeepney, the motorcycle-powered tricycle, and the engine-powered kuliglig, the open-air pedicab provides shade when needed.

Photo by:
Michael J. Alsup

Photo by:
Michael J. Alsup

Most active volcano in the
Philippines

MAYON

The volcano with its surrounding landscape was declared a national park on July 20, 1938, the first in the nation. It was reclassified as a Natural Park and renamed as the Mayon Volcano Natural Park in 2000.[6] It is the centerpiece of the Albay Biosphere Reserve, declared by UNESCO in 2016,[7] and is currently being nominated as a World Heritage Site.

https://en.wikipedia.org/wiki/Mayon

"Traveling to another part of the world opened up a passion with photography. Photographing people in another culture and in which they live was not only intriguing, but it led me to the inspiration of writing. "

Michael J. Alsup

About the author*:*
Place: Torrence, California
Currently resides in Beaumont TX

Memberships:
Beaumont Camera Club
Texas Gulf Coast Writers Group
Philippine Association of Beaumont TX

coming this winter

If you enjoyed Michael J. Alsup's
"Miracles Are Chosen",
be sure to look for the sequel to this story:

IDOLS OF ENDEAVOR

If you have any comments, please
submit to publisher's email address:

Coastal Winds Publishing House
Port Arthur, Texas
Email:publisher@coastalwindspublishinghouse.co

CPSIA information can be obtained
at www.ICGtesting.com
Printed in the USA
BVHW011747130820
586335BV00003B/55